THE
DUKE
AND THE

Assassin

THE
ROYAL AGENTS
OF
MI6

BOOK ONE

USA TODAY BESTSELLING AUTHOR

HEATHER SLADE

THE DUKE AND THE ASSASSIN
© 2021 Heather Slade

This book is a work of fiction. The names, characters, places and incidents are products of the writer's imagination or have been used fictitiously and are not to be construed as real. Any resemblance to persons, living or dead, actual events, locale or organizations is entirely coincidental.

Paperback:
ISBN: 978-1-953626-31-8

MORE FROM AUTHOR HEATHER SLADE

Table of Contents

1

Shiver

"Thornton, are you listening?"

I turned away from the window where I'd been looking out at the dormant gardens of Whittaker Abbey. The land had been handed down, heir to heir, since 1547 when the former Cistern abbey was taken over by Henry VIII. Shortly afterward, the estate was given to John Whittaker as a gift from the king for his service.

As a boy, I'd explored every acre of the forested estate and its gardens, knowing that one day, the care and maintenance of the land would be my responsibility. It had seemed a long way off then—not until I was an old man, when my father, the fourteenth Duke, passed away.

Until then, I would remain the Marquess of Wells and, more importantly to me, a high-ranking agent in the United Kingdom's Secret Intelligence Service, also known as Military Intelligence Section 6, or MI6.

"I beg your pardon, Duchess," I answered, looking lovingly at my mother, the woman who had been the guiding force of our family in the months since my father had suffered a debilitating stroke.

"What news of Sutton?"

Like me, my younger brother by two years, known to most as Wilder, was employed by Her Majesty's Secret Service. However, he was on the national security side—MI5.

I sneaked a look at my phone. "He's expected this afternoon."

"Very good. You and he will get the trees."

My first thought was to ask why the groundskeepers couldn't handle it on their own, as they'd had even before my father's illness, but I understood my mother was grasping for any semblance of what she considered normalcy. Choosing the trees that would be brought into the abbey and decorated for the holidays was something my father, brother, and I had done together until I'd turned eighteen and left for university.

"We will do," I muttered, wondering how many trees my mother planned to decorate this year. Was more than one really necessary? It wasn't as though she would entertain this holiday season.

Duchess Victoria was the eldest daughter of the Duke and Duchess of Cumberland and still practiced what some believed to be archaic traditions of the English nobility.

"Come, sit with me," she said, holding her hand out to me. "Tell me what's troubling you."

I sat, but had no intention of confiding in her. I also had no intention of lying, so chose not to say anything.

"Have you seen your father this morning?" she asked.

"I read the news to him."

My mother patted my hand. "You know how much he likes to catch up over his morning tea."

I doubted my father had heard a word I read, and he'd certainly not had any tea, but as the doctors had told us, the important thing was that the family spent time with him and conversed whether the duke was able to respond or not.

"There's more," she murmured.

"What's that?"

"Something is on your mind, Thornton, and whatever it is, its weight is heavy."

Even if I wanted to discuss it with my mother, I wouldn't know where to begin.

"It's a woman."

I leaned closer. "It's nothing," I said softly. "Let it be, Duchess."

"For now," she said, standing and leaning down to kiss my cheek. "I'll check on your father."

I nodded and stood too, walking back over to the window.

It had been over a month since United Russia lifted the ten-million-dollar bounty they had on Orina "Losha" Kuznetsov's head, and yet I had no idea where she was and why she insisted on staying so far underground that no one could find her.

I'd called in every favor—and there had been many—but so far, I didn't have a single lead as to where the bloody woman was hiding.

"You best be driving in the gate," I said when I answered my brother's call a couple of hours later.

Wilder laughed. "At least an hour out, but before you blast me, I've spent the last thirty minutes listening to Sir Ranald tell me how he intends to fire you."

I laughed too. "My Christmas wish come true."

"What the bloody hell did you do?"

The memory of it made me cringe.

***

I pounded my fist on the desk of the office I'd been holed up in, cursing the impotence I felt as much as the walls surrounding me.

Ten minutes ago, my boss had summoned me, but I wasn't any closer to giving him the answer he sought than I had been two weeks ago when Rivet had first asked for my decision.

Sir Ranald "Rivet" Caird was a career British Intelligence officer for MI6 who, nine years prior, had been named chief. At the time, he'd been candid about his refusal to serve beyond a ten-year term.

The first in line to succeed him had been Merrigan Shaw, who was now Merrigan Shaw-Butler, happily married to Kade "Doc" Butler, the founding partner of the private security and intelligence firm made up primarily of former CIA operatives—K19 Security Solutions. Merrigan had taken over as managing partner of the firm and had made it perfectly clear that she wouldn't return to MI6 regardless of the position offered.

As much as that had infuriated our boss, Rivet had seen her departure coming in the same way I had, and couldn't begrudge her the happiness she and Doc had in their lives.

With Merrigan out of the picture, I'd moved to the top spot to succeed Sir Ranald. My lack of enthusiasm, along with my refusal to give the man an answer, incensed my boss.

"He's pacing," said Patsy, sticking her head in my office. "Would you mind?"

"In a minute," I snapped, immediately regretting my tone. Patsy was Rivet's assistant and didn't deserve my or anyone else's wrath.

"I take it you haven't heard anything."

Patsy was well aware of my search for Losha Kuznetsov, and had done everything she could to help. While her level of security clearance was high or higher than mine, she couldn't do too much digging without getting in trouble with Rivet herself.

"Sorry, Pats. Not your fault or your problem."

"Go talk to him. Get it over with so we can all start enjoying the holiday."

"I hadn't thought of that," I muttered, cursing myself again for my thoughtlessness.

Patsy motioned with her head toward Rivet's office, and I stood.

"You're not a duke yet," Rivet barked when I walked in. "Until you are, I outrank you, and I expect you to respond appropriately."

"Yes, sir. My apologies."

"The resources of the Secret Intelligence Service are not yours to make use of for personal matters."

"Understood." Now wasn't the time to argue with Rivet, but other than making contact with several of our operatives, I hadn't used SIS "resources" to search for Kuznetsov.

"That being said, I am authorizing a fact-finding mission."

"Don't."

Rivet raised an eyebrow.

"I'm not ready to give you an answer."

"You're under the assumption that I'm authorizing the mission in exchange for your acceptance of the position?"

"To a certain extent."

"Get the hell out of my office! In fact, get the hell out of the building."

"Rivet, I meant no—"

"*Out!*"

***

At the end of my recount, my brother laughed. "Did you wish him a happy Christmas on your way out?"

I ran my hand through my hair. "He's frustrated that I won't give him an answer."

"No, Shiver, he's pissed off that you thought so little of him," he said, referring to me by the code name used by most outside my family.

When my brother didn't say anything else, I thought perhaps our call had dropped, but then I heard him take a deep breath.

"We'll find her, but in the meantime, you have to find a way to compartmentalize."

If my brother were standing in front of me, I'd likely belt him, after which I'd feel equally as guilty as I did about my conversation with Rivet. However, I had no restraint despite knowing I'd experience regret.

"Where the hell is she?" I said in a way I wouldn't to anyone but my brother.

"I wish I had the answer, Shiv."

2

Losha

I looked into the most beautiful deep gray eyes that had ever graced the universe. Kazmir wasn't just the heavens' most beloved angel given to me as a precious gift; he was my world, and I would do anything to protect him.

"What shall we do today?" I whispered, kissing the baby's brow.

Kazmir cooed and gave me one of the sweet smiles I craved.

I'd been in hiding since I first discovered I was pregnant, fearful that United Russia, the modern-day iteration of the KGB and the current ruling party of the country, would force me to terminate it.

Shortly after I disappeared, my UR handler discovered the affair I'd been having with MI6 agent Thornton "Shiver" Whittaker and openly accused me of being a double agent. Thus, a bounty had been placed on my head and my assets had been frozen.

I'd been prepared for it, though. I'd been planning my defection—because, in essence, that's what it was—for over two years, knowing the accusation was inevitable.

The burner cell I kept near the bedside table vibrated, and I ran to grab it.

"Ovsyanaya kasha," a woman's voice said. My oldest and dearest friend, Zaryana Ivashov, and I had agreed on the code phrase years ago to identify ourselves to one another.

While Zary was the only person who had the phone's number, I wasn't foolish enough to think it would stay that way. United Russia's reach was global, and eventually, regardless of what fail-safes I put in place, they'd find me.

"Hello, Zary," I responded. "How are you?"

"I'm worried about you, Losha."

The code name Zary called me by was one my friend had given me years ago. She'd told me at the time that my long dark hair looked as beautiful as a horse's mane.

We'd met when the then-KGB took us and several other teenage girls from the orphanages we were living in, and trained us to be spies.

"Orina, please tell me where you are," Zary pleaded. "You don't need to hide anymore. The bounty has been lifted."

I could hear the desperation in my friend's voice and understood I would've felt the same way if the situations were reversed.

If it were just my life at risk, maybe I would've believed the words of the only person worthy of my trust when she assured me again and again that I no longer had to stay in hiding. As it was, I couldn't be too careful.

"It is difficult for me to believe that United Russia would give up so easily."

"It wasn't easily, Losha. Shiver—"

From the other room, Kazmir began to cry as though he'd heard Zary's words and understood the pain they brought me.

While I immediately ended the call, I knew it hadn't been quickly enough. Zary had to have heard the baby's cry.

I was about to park in front of my rented flat after running some errands when the hair on the back of my neck stood on end. Danger was close; I felt it on every nerve ending.

That the day would come, was inevitable; my only question was, who? Had United Russia found me, or had Shiver?

I looked in the rearview mirror at the beautiful baby sleeping peacefully in the backseat. As hard as it would be to leave the sweet flat we'd called home since shortly after Kazmir was born, we had no choice. *Someone* had found us, signaling it was time for us to move on.

My only regret was not being able to spend the upcoming holiday in Lapland. After being almost entirely destroyed during World War II, the region had rebuilt, proclaiming itself the official home of Father Christmas. Spending the holiday here was more for me than my son; Kazmir wouldn't remember anything of our temporary home.

I turned the car around and was about to drive away, when I recognized a man getting out of another SUV.

Axel "Pinch" Fulton. His presence meant three things. Shiver Whittaker was either with him or not far behind; SIS was likely involved in my manhunt; and any hesitation I might have felt over leaving was long gone, like I soon would be.

"I'm in the States, and…I need help," I said when I called Zary three days later.

"Where in the States are you?"

"DC."

"Tell me what you need, Losha."

"A place to stay. At least temporarily." My eyes filled with tears looking at my sleeping baby. We'd spent the last two nights in different motels, and the change in surroundings was affecting Kazmir's sleep. I needed to find a place we could stay for several nights in a row.

"Let me see what I can do."

"You can't tell anyone."

"I have to tell Gunner." Zary sighed.

"Why?"

"I can't help you on my own anymore, Losha. I don't have the resources."

"Never mind, then."

"Wait. Don't hang up."

I sighed like Zary had. "What?"

"I trust him. If I ask him not to tell anyone where you are, he won't."

I didn't know what to say. Could I dare trust a man I'd never met based solely on Zary's opinion? Gunner was a former CIA operative, and along with being Zary's fiancé, he was a partner in a private intelligence and security firm that Shiver had connections to.

Again, I faced the same dilemma. If it were only me, I could afford to take the risk, but Kazmir's life was at stake too.

"I heard the baby's cry," said Zary. "Let me help you."

"I'll call you back." I abruptly ended the call.

I looked around the dank and dark motel room. Not knowing when or how I'd be able to generate an income again, I was hesitant to spend any more money than necessary. I'd stockpiled as much cash as I could without drawing attention to it. If UR had noticed, they would've been onto my plan before I'd had time to put everything in place.

Zary had admitted she heard the baby crying; maybe she'd already told Gunner.

A few minutes later, I called her back. "I need help. If you must tell Gunner, I'll have to accept that. If there is any way you can help me without doing so, I'd consider it a personal favor."

"A personal favor? Losha, you saved my life. Countless times, in fact. Don't you realize I would do anything for you?"

The emotion in my one and only friend's voice brought me to tears. "Thank you," I whispered.

"I asked you before to give me a couple of hours. Are you able to, or do you need to move immediately?"

"I'll be okay for a few days."

"It won't take that long. Is there anything else you need me to do right now?"

"Just that…"

"What is it?"

"The baby…"

"No one will know except Gunner and me."

"Thank you," I whispered a second time.

3

Shiver

"Three trees? Is this really necessary?" complained Wilder.

I nodded in response.

"Have you been in to see the duke this morning?"

Neither my father nor my mother had ever suggested my brother or I call them Duke and Duchess; it was just something we'd started doing when we were teenagers. Our sister, Darrow, hadn't followed suit and still called them Mother and Father.

"I see him every morning, Wild."

"He doesn't look good."

I helped Wellie, the head groundskeeper who had been part of our lives since my brother, sister, and I were children, load the first of the trees into the back of the estate wagon.

What did Wild expect me to say? Our father as we'd known him was gone. In his place was a man who couldn't speak, eat on his own, or get himself up to use the toilet. The effects of the series of strokes he'd had, had left him a shell of his former self.

As much as I knew better, I still prayed the duke wasn't fully aware of his deteriorated condition. It was the only way I could cope with looking into my father's haunted eyes each morning. If I thought those eyes were imploring me to end his suffering, the guilt of being unable to do so would eat me alive.

"Good morning, lass," said Wellie, breaking me out of my reverie.

The three of us had started calling Alcott Fulton "Wellie" when we were children, given we'd never seen the man wear any footwear besides Wellington boots.

"Good morning," said Darrow, kissing the old man's cheek. "These wankers couldn't chop down trees on their own?" she asked before walking over to hug first Wilder and then me.

"Mind your tongue," said Wellie, but with a smile that conveyed the love he had for the woman who had always been like a daughter to him.

"Axel is trying to reach you," she whispered in my ear.

I pulled out my mobile and saw I'd missed two calls and a text.

"Excuse me," I said to her, Wilder, and Wellie.

"Tell me something worthwhile," I said when the man my sister called Axel but most everyone else referred to as Pinch, answered my call.

"The news is good and bad."

"Get on with it."

"She was here, but it appears we just missed her."

"Where?"

"Rovani."

What in the bloody hell was she doing in Lapland, Finland, at this time of year when it was rarely warmer than minus twenty Celsius?

"There's more."

"Go on, Pinch."

"It doesn't appear she's alone."

I closed my eyes. The stabbing pain I experienced just thinking about Losha, intensified to the equivalent of a hundred blades. Is this why she refused to surface, refused to make contact? Had she found someone else? The idea of it filled me with as much sorrow as rage. How could she? In the span of a few months, she'd moved on?

The idea of it would have been ludicrous delivered by anyone other than Pinch. The man, who happened to be Wellie's only child, was like a fourth sibling, not just to me, but to Wilder and Darrow too.

"Shiv?"

"Yeah. I'm here."

"I'm not sure you understand. The neighbor reported seeing a child. Not a child really—a baby."

The muscles in my abdomen clenched. A baby? It couldn't be hers; Losha had been sterilized by the KGB when she was eighteen. Although, the KGB had certainly been known to lie. In fact, I'd heard through intel circles that the fiancée of a good friend of his, a woman Losha had been recruited and trained with, was currently pregnant.

"Who's the man?"

"What man?"

"The one she's with."

"I never said anything about a man."

"I'm not following."

"Those we questioned failed to mention anyone other than the woman and her baby."

"No one else?"

"That's right."

"Flipping hell," I muttered, running my hand through my hair. "I need to find her."

"On it, Shiv. Sorry I missed her."

"I'll work it on this end. At least we know where she's traveling from. In the meantime, get your arse home."

"I'm not coming home for the holiday this year."

I walked farther away. "I'm with your father as we speak."

"He's aware."

"If this is about Losha—"

"It's not."

"If I find out otherwise…"

"I swear on my father's life it's not. How's that?"

I cringed. *"Jesus,* Pinch."

"I'll be in touch."

I heard the familiar sound of the call ending and wished I could continue walking away. I needed time on my own to think.

"Everything okay?" Darrow approached and asked.

"Yes, fine," I snapped.

"Was your call about Father?"

I reached out and put my arm around my sister's shoulders; she looked as though she was about to cry. "No, nothing to do with the duke."

She pulled back and looked into my eyes.

"I promise."

"I haven't been to see him yet this morning."

I kissed her forehead. "Go on, then."

She waved behind her as she walked away.

"Where's she off to?" asked Wilder.

"To see the duke."

"What's wrong?"

"As I told her, nothing. She hasn't been up to the house yet this morning."

Darrow lived on the estate in one of the smaller residences, called Covington House. I laughed to myself. Being away from home for so long and then being back again skewed my perspective. The ten-thousand-square-foot home was hardly small.

"Not with the duke; with you. Was the call about Losha?"

I looked away. "It was."

"And?"

I turned back and met my brother's eyes. "Do you think you can handle getting the other two trees on your own?"

Wilder studied me. "Definitely," he said giving me a half-hearted shove.

"We'll talk later."

Rather than going back to the main house, I kept walking.

Pinch hadn't said how old the baby was, and I hadn't asked. If the intel he'd collected was accurate, that Losha had a child with her, it explained why she'd remained underground. I wondered who the father was, if the baby was, in fact, hers. Was he in the picture? Just because Pinch hadn't seen or heard about a man from the neighbors he'd questioned, didn't mean there wasn't one.

"Every flight out of every airport remotely close to Lapland, Finland—every flight out of Europe. I don't care what it costs, Doc. I can't run this through SIS," I said to the man who was one of my oldest and dearest friends. He had been since Doc Butler was a green CIA agent and I was a greener MI6 operative. We'd worked together so many times, I'd lost count.

"Understood. Be specific about what we're looking for."

"A couple traveling with a baby. Either that or a woman and a baby."

"Traveling at the holidays?"

"I get it. Needle in a haystack." I knew exactly what I was asking of Doc. "As I said, no matter the cost."

"This could get very expensive, Shiv. It's the week before Christmas."

"I'm well aware." How could I explain that I had to know? Whomever Losha was with, whomever the baby's father was, I had to know.

"It isn't just the monetary cost, Shiv. What about the personal one, and by that, I mean to you?"

"What I said before stands. No matter the cost. I have to know where she is."

"And if I said no?"

"I'd call Merrigan."

Doc laughed as did I. As far back as he and I went, Merrigan and I had known each other longer, since university. If Doc didn't assign a team to this, his wife would make bloody well sure he did.

"How's your father?"

"Not well. Thank you for asking. I can't leave England presently."

"I'm sorry, Shiv, and I understand. I'll bring the team up to speed and will keep you posted on our progress."

"I appreciate it."

An hour passed before I returned to the main house to find the duchess, Darrow, and Wilder having tea in our mother's favorite drawing room.

"Come, Thornton," she said, waving me over.

When my eyes met Wilder's, I knew my brother recognized my worry.

"Hey, Shiv. Fancy a trip to town?" he asked.

I didn't miss our mother's frown at my brother's use of what she considered an inappropriate "nickname."

"Why do you need to go to town?" asked Darrow.

"Bit of shopping to do," Wilder answered without looking at her.

"For?"

"Darrow, please."

Our sister scowled at him. "You're both so secretive."

"It's the nature of the job, dear sister," said Wilder, putting his arm around her shoulders.

"This has nothing to do with 'the job,' and you both know it."

"No need to pout. It's Christmas after all," I reminded her.

She laughed. "I don't believe whatever secrets you're keeping have anything to do with Christmas either."

She was right, not that either Wilder or I would tell her so.

"Excuse me a moment," said our mother, leaving the room.

"What news of Axel?" Darrow asked once she was certain the duchess was out of earshot.

"He said he won't be home for the holidays this year," I answered. "Why do you ask?"

When she murmured, "Just curious," I looked at Wilder, who raised his eyebrow.

"I saw that," she said between sips of tea. "You aren't the only ones with secrets, you know."

Wilder laughed out loud. "Are you suggesting that you and Axel have a secret?"

Darrow shrugged a shoulder.

"What are the three of you discussing?" our mother asked, rejoining us.

"I'm not certain, but I think it might involve a secret romance," answered Wilder, winking at our sister, who stuck her tongue out at him.

"Is there a chance any of the three of you will ever give me grandchildren? And Thornton, I remind you, the responsibility of an heir rests on your shoulders."

I inwardly cringed at both of my mother's comments. That she was anxious for grandchildren only served as a reminder that Losha may have had a child with another man, as did her comment about producing an heir. Not that I held the same line of thinking as my mother. These weren't the dark ages. My brother or sister could take over the estate at any time. In fact, it was something I wanted to discuss with them while Wilder and I were home for the holiday.

"One day, Duchess, I'm sure one of us will make you a grandmum—"

"What do you say?" asked Wilder, abruptly standing and motioning toward the door.

His reaction was puzzling. I waited for him to say more, and when he didn't, I stood and walked over to our mother. "We'll be back soon, Duchess," I said, leaning down to kiss her cheek.

She smiled and nodded, focusing her attention back on Darrow. "Your sister can keep me company."

I almost laughed out loud at Darrow's scowl.

"What was that all about? I mean I was joking, and then the duchess went straight to 'when are you going to give me grandkids,'" asked Wilder, climbing into the passenger seat of my vintage Austin-Healey 3000 MK III. The British racing green convertible with a classic tan interior had originally belonged to our father. When I left for university, the duke had gifted it to me, to the great disappointment of both Wilder and Darrow, who had each assumed the car would one day belong to them. "You don't think Darrow's really having a tryst with Pinch…"

"I don't know, Wild. It seems unlikely."

"They're like siblings."

I shrugged. "And yet, they're not."

Wilder shuddered. "He wouldn't."

There were plenty of people whom I might've once thought the same thing about. I never would've thought Losha would walk out of my life, only to have a child with another man, either.

"Do you actually need to go to town?"

Wilder nodded. "I haven't done a lick of shopping for the holiday, have you?"

I shook my head. I'd never been big on Christmas. Too often I'd attempted to use the excuse of a mission to get out of the annual family gathering. It had rarely worked. Somehow, my mother had easily ascertained whether I was actually required to be away or not.

"Fancy a stop at the pub first? The duchess insisted on tea when I would've much preferred a pint."

"A baby?" asked Wilder after we'd gone through more than one pint.

"That's what Pinch said."

"If it had been anyone but him…"

"I thought the same thing."

"And you're not the father?"

"I'm not." I'd briefly considered the possibility, but we'd never failed to use protection, plus, why would she remain in hiding, refusing to get in touch with me if the child were mine?

"How can you be so certain?"

"I'm certain."

"I'm sorry, Shiv."

"Me too."

4

Losha

"Gunner will meet you at the ferry in Deale, unless you would like him to come and get you," Zary told me a few hours later.

"No, I have transport. Where is it he's taking me?"

"A private island in the Chesapeake Bay."

"You can't be serious."

"I am. And wait until you see the house. It's amazing. But more importantly, it's completely private."

"Who owns it?"

"Gunner does."

If my predicament wasn't so desperate, I might've laughed. "This sounds too good to be true."

"I know, but, Losha, it isn't. Gunner promised me he won't tell anyone you're there, or even that he's seen you. He won't break his promise to me."

"I don't know how to thank you."

"You're family. No thanks needed."

My eyes filled with tears. I didn't begrudge my friend every happiness, but I found myself envying her. Gunner would do anything for Zary.

There would be no knight in shining armor coming to my rescue. I had Kazmir though, and my son made up for everything else lacking in my life.

"After the holiday, I'll come see you. If you want me to."

"Of course I do. I'm sorry if I've made you think I don't trust you. It's just…"

"I understand and I'll see you soon. Happy Christmas, Losha."

"Happy Christmas," I answered, wondering how it possibly could be.

When Gunner pulled up in an SUV and parked next to me, I was relieved to see he'd come alone, as promised.

I slowly got out of the car and waited for him to approach.

"I'm Gunner Godet," he said, not coming any closer until I responded.

"Thank you for meeting me."

Gunner took a few more steps. "What do you have with you? Did Zary tell you there are no cars on the island?"

"Yes." I peeked at Kazmir, who was thankfully still asleep, before walking to the back of the car and opening the trunk.

"Zary mentioned that you aren't traveling alone." Gunner pointed to my bags. "May I?"

"Yes. Thank you." I watched him lug the two suitcases and the baby's travel crib from the trunk. I opened the back door and unhooked the car seat from its base. If there were no cars on the island, I wouldn't need the complete setup.

"Who is this?" Gunner asked in a whisper, smiling when I followed him to the dock.

"This is Kazmir," I whispered too even though the baby had woken up and was peering at me.

"He's beautiful."

Most of the baby was covered by blankets, but his gray eyes and curly dark hair were visible. "Thank you."

He stopped and looked into my eyes. "I've hired a boat to take you over myself. It means we don't have help, but it also means that no one other than myself and Zary know you and your baby are on the island."

"Thank you. I…" I looked away, unable to finish my sentence. Relying on others had never been easy for me.

"Listen, Zary told me how you looked out for her. She's my life, which means, I owe you my life."

"I find myself at a loss for words with both you and Zary. Thank you seems so inadequate."

"No thanks required. Let's go. It's only going to get colder out on the water."

The boat he hired was over thirty feet in length and had an enclosed cabin.

"Have a seat." Gunner motioned near what looked like controls and a steering wheel. "I'll load everything else on."

"What is all that?" I asked when he made more than one trip back from his vehicle, carrying boxes with him.

"Provisions."

"Oh, I—"

Gunner held up his hand. "I haven't stocked the house in several weeks, and it needed to be done."

"I didn't think about it," I said, feeling foolish and careless and like a terrible mother. I was so worried about keeping Kazmir a secret that I wasn't thinking about the basic necessities of what he and I needed.

"Listen. I don't know much about babies or having them, but I do know that it's gotta be one of the hardest things in life."

"And the best."

Gunner smiled. "I guess I'll know soon enough."

I gasped. "Is Zary pregnant?"

Gunner nodded. "She is."

"I'm so happy for her, and you. We didn't think…"

"She said that the KGB told you both that you wouldn't be able to have children."

"Stupid on their part to tell women they couldn't have children. Did they think that would mean we wouldn't have sex?"

"You make a good point. Although my guess is your handlers, trainers, whatever you called them, were misogynistic enough not to consider unprotected sex."

"Anyway, please pass on my congratulations."

"I know she wanted to be here tonight, but it likely would've raised questions."

"Understood."

Gunner untied the boat and slowly maneuvered it away from the dock. "It'll take about twenty minutes to get there. I have a golf cart near the landing. It's covered, but it will still be chilly."

"Thank you. Zary told me you're a good man."

"I don't know if many people would agree with you about that."

"She wouldn't love you if you weren't."

He smiled. "I'm a lucky man."

I smiled too, but it faded quickly as I thought about the man I loved. He was a good man too, but that didn't mean he would easily forgive my betrayal.

5

Shiver

"That was painful," said Wilder when he, Darrow, and I came back into the drawing room after saying good night to our mother.

"Worst Christmas ever," whispered my sister, sharing the sentiment we all felt.

Between our father's illness, and the general lack of holiday spirit among us, the day had dragged on endlessly.

"How long are you home?" Darrow asked.

"I don't yet know, sweet pea." I rarely used the name I'd called her since she was a toddler.

She turned to Wilder. "What about you?"

"I'm going to stick around home for a while."

I raised a brow.

"It's my turn," mumbled Wilder.

The last thing I wanted was for my siblings to feel as though they needed to take on responsibilities that were mine, but in this case, if I heard anything more about Losha's whereabouts, I wanted to be able to leave at a moment's notice.

"Appreciate it," I muttered.

"What's going on?" Darrow asked.

"Work," Wilder answered for me.

"Tell me when you're leaving," Darrow said again, this time more demanding.

"As I said, I don't know yet." I studied her. "Why?"

She looked away and stared at something outside the window.

"Darrow?" I said again, resting my hand on her shoulder.

"You'll think I'm terrible," she whispered.

I pulled her to me and hugged her. "No one is going to begrudge you a break. Is that what will make Wild and me think you're terrible?"

She nodded. "I'm sorry."

"Don't be," said Wilder, pulling her into a hug like I had. "That's why I'm sticking around."

I sensed there was something else going on with Darrow, but as fragile as she seemed, I wouldn't ask. "There's something else unrelated I'd like to discuss with you both."

"Go on, then," said Wilder, releasing Darrow from his embrace.

"Not here."

"Too cold for a walk," said Darrow. "Although I'm worried about Wellie."

I was too. We'd invited the man to the house to celebrate with the family, but he'd declined. Even with all of Darrow's pleading, he wouldn't give in.

"Let's pay him a visit," Wilder suggested. "It isn't too cold for a drive."

"What did you want to talk to us about?" Wilder asked as we approached Wellie's cottage.

"The management of the estate. For now, the duchess is overseeing most of the day-to-day business on a purely tertiary basis, but I'd like to discuss hiring a full-time manager."

"That's your decision," said Darrow.

"That's the other thing I wanted to discuss. The estate as a whole was put into a trust by our great-grandfather. While the duke's trust is now irrevocable since he is in failing health, upon his passing, mine will not be."

"What are you getting at?" Wilder asked.

"I'd like to divide the estate equally between the three of us. It won't mean much in the short term as the income will be used solely for our mother's care and the upkeep of the buildings and grounds. However, upon her passing, the three of us would become equal partners, unless one or all of us would prefer to be bought out. In that case, we'd have to discuss whether any of us want to hold on to the property, or sell it outright."

"You can't be serious," said Darrow. "Sell Whittaker Abbey?"

"I'm not saying definitively. Only if none of the three of us wants to live here and manage it."

"You're giving up your birthright," said Wilder.

"I'm not saying that either. What I'm saying is that it isn't just my inheritance. It should be divided equally."

"Why?" Darrow asked.

"Because we live in the twenty-first century. I should not inherit it all, leaving the two of you nothing of your own birthright."

"Have you discussed this with the duchess?"

I shook my head. "I have not, and I don't intend to."

"I see. You think she'll forbid it."

"Actually, Wild, it isn't any of her business, and for that reason alone, I want the trust to be handled in the way I'm suggesting."

"I don't follow."

I motioned toward the backseat. "Darrow is entitled to this inheritance just as much as you or I are. The fact that she can't inherit because she's a woman is as ludicrous as you not being able to inherit because you were second born."

"I doubt I'd be so generous," Wilder muttered.

"You would be."

My two siblings were quiet when I pulled up in front of Wellie's cottage.

I opened the boot and handed Wilder the basket of food we'd asked the kitchen staff to prepare. Darrow, it seemed, was already inside the house.

"Are you sure about this, Shiv?"

"The estate trust?"

He nodded.

"Absolutely. Without any hesitation. Come on, then, let's share some Christmas cheer with Wellie."

More than a week later, I heard from both Doc and Pinch within one hour of each other.

"I was certain it was them, and then facial recognition confirmed Orina's identity," said Pinch. "I'll forward the footage to you now."

"Doc said a member of the K19 team spotted her at Reagan too."

"How close do you want me to get?" he asked.

"Let me get back to you with an answer. I have to sort things out here, but if I can, I'll fly out tomorrow."

"How's the duke?"

"No real change. The doctors have said he could linger in this state for months."

"I'm sorry, Shiv."

"I appreciate it. By the way, we spent some time with your father on Christmas."

"He told me. He said Darrow stayed on after you and Wilder left."

"He's like a second father to her. I sometimes think she spent more time with Wellie than the duke and duchess combined."

Pinch muttered something that I didn't catch, but it didn't seem important.

"I'll be in touch, and thanks, Pinch. I know you're doing this on your own time. I hope your father's health doesn't suffer for it."

"I had other reasons for not coming home, Shiv."

"Does that mean you didn't lie to me when you said you weren't staying away because of Losha?"

"I swore on my father's life, Shiv."

After ending the call, I went in search of my brother. This was the news I'd been waiting for, and now that I knew Losha was in the States, I was compelled to go to her.

"Where are you?" I asked when Wilder answered my call.

"With Darrow, at Covington House."

Good, they were together. "I'll be right there."

First, though, I needed to talk to the duchess, whom I found reading in her drawing room.

"Thornton," she said, holding her hand out to me.

"Duchess, I'm afraid I have to leave."

She nodded, as though she'd expected the news.

"Wilder will be staying on here for some time."

"Sit, Thornton," she said, pointing to the chair nearest her. "Tell me what's really going on with you."

"Mother—"

"Oh, dear. You haven't called me that since you were a child. Now I know it's really something. It's a woman, isn't it, Thornton?"

What could I do other than smile? "Yes, Duchess."

"I'm not letting you leave until you tell me the whole story."

I could never tell her the whole story even if I wanted to. Too much of my history with Losha was woven into both United Russia and SIS.

"Thornton…"

"She's someone I care a great deal about, Duchess."

"Does she return the sentiment?"

"There was a time I thought so."

"And now?"

"I don't know."

She nodded and smiled in that way mothers do. "You need to know."

I nodded in return. "One way or another."

"When are you leaving?" Darrow asked before I could close her front door behind me.

"In the morning."

"I want to go with you."

I raised a brow.

"Sutton told me this isn't a SIS deal."

I glared at Wild, who laughed.

"I did no such thing, you little imp." He looked at me. "She's fishing."

"You're going to the States though, right?"

"I am, but if Wilder didn't divulge that information, I'd like to know who did."

"It doesn't matter. I have…friends in DC, and you and Sutton agreed that I shouldn't feel ashamed to say I need a break."

I caught her hesitation and wondered why she really wanted to go to Washington. If it were as simple as having friends there, Wilder and I would know their entire life story by now. It wasn't like Darrow not to be specific to the point of tedium.

"I can book the flight," she offered.

"I'll handle it."

"I can—"

"No. You can't. As I said, I'll handle it. Where do these friends live? If you let me know, I can also arrange for a place for you to stay."

"I'm not a child, Thornton. I can make my own travel arrangements."

"I'm going to interject and tell you that if you allow Shiver to do it, you'll fly first class and your accommodations will be as impressive," said Wilder.

"I don't care about that."

He looked at me and was about to laugh, but I shook my head. Something was up with Darrow, and whatever it was, she wasn't being honest about it. Which meant there was something she was hiding.

Darrow slept the majority of the flight from London to Washington, DC, not that it would've been easy to converse once we'd each settled into the first-class sleeping pods.

"Sutton was right about the perks of traveling with you," she said, pulling the cashmere blanket up to her chin right before she nodded off. "Thank you, Thornton."

I smiled. "Get some sleep, sweet pea."

I ran my hand through my hair, wishing sleep would come as easily to me as it did to my sister. Too much weighed heavily on my mind—all of which had to do with Losha.

I was torn between what I believed might be the right thing to do and what I was compelled to do instead. Did

I have any right to question her about whether she was in a relationship with another man—one with whom she had a child? Was it any of my business? Hadn't she made it clear when we were last together that we had no future?

The bottom line was, I'd believed Losha loved me. I believed we were meant to be together. And finally, whether she loved me or not, I loved her. If she had moved on, if there was another man in her life, if they were starting a family, my heart would be irrevocably broken—but I still had to know.

6

Losha

I walked the floor of Gunner's house, wishing I could fall asleep regardless of time zone, like I used to be able to. Since giving birth to Kazmir, my body resisted sleep no matter how exhausted I felt. It was four in the morning, and I wasn't the slightest bit sleepy.

Opening the door to the pantry, I was happy to see several boxes of tea sitting on the shelf near the coffee. I added water to the kettle sitting on the stove.

When I spoke to Zary about Gunner's house, I hadn't known what to think, but this place would've far exceeded any expectation I might've had.

The four-bedroom structure sat in a clearing, surrounded by tall trees. While it had every modern convenience, the outside of it looked as though it had been on the island forever—not in age, but in the way it seemed to rise from the earth as if it belonged there.

When Gunner had explained there weren't any coverings on the windows since it was a private island, it seemed logical. However, walking around the lit house when it was dark outside was something that would take me time to get used to.

I tiptoed into the bedroom where Kazmir was sound asleep in his portable crib. I could spend hours looking at my precious baby boy. Never in my wildest dreams had I ever thought I'd be a mother.

It was one of countless reasons I'd told Shiver that a relationship between us could never work. When we'd argued about it the last time I saw him, I never could've predicted that a few short weeks after that, I'd find out I was pregnant.

***

"Where are you going?" Shiver grumbled when I got out of bed.

"I'll be right back." I leaned in to kiss him.

Instead, he grabbed me, rolled me over, and eased my legs open with his knee.

I looked into his green-gray eyes as he brought his lips to mine and pushed his hardness against my sex. He reached over to the nightstand, grabbed a foil packet, and sheathed himself.

His powerful arms rested near my shoulders as he thrust inside me, his gaze so intense that it almost brought me to tears. I closed my eyes and turned my head, unable to bear the idea of what he might be thinking, and knowing I'd never be enough for him.

"I love—"

"Don't."

When I put my fingers to his lips, he nipped and then licked them. "I love you, Losha."

It wasn't the first time he'd said it, and still, I couldn't say the words back to him.

"Shiv—"

"The only words I want to hear you say are that you love me too. Otherwise, don't speak."

I smiled and closed my eyes when he thrust into me again and again. My fingernails dug into his skin as he brought me to another orgasm. I'd lost count of how many times he had in the last twenty-four hours.

Shiver rolled to my side and circled my hardened nipple with the tip of his finger. "Come away with me," he murmured, bringing his mouth to my breast. "Come." *Nip.* "Away." *Another nip.* "With me."

"I can't," I groaned and writhed against him.

"Come to Bedfordshire."

I moved away from him and sat up, pulling the sheet over my body. "No."

Shiver tugged it out of my hands. "Why not?"

"How many times do we have to have this conversation?"

"As many times as necessary until I convince you."

I grabbed the sheet from him as he'd done to me. "We don't have that kind of relationship, Shiver."

"We don't?" He kissed his way up my arm to my neck and nibbled under my ear. "I can't get enough of you," he groaned. "Come away with me."

I shrugged away from him and stood. "I have to go."

Shiver stood too. "No, you don't." He wrapped his arms around my waist. "We still have another twenty-four hours, and for once, I want to have this conversation without you leaving in the midst of it."

I grabbed the robe I'd thrown on the chair the night before and put it on, although it didn't stop him from putting his arms around me again or from nuzzling my neck.

"Come on, Losha. Tell me why not."

"I've just said why not. I'm not the kind of woman you take home to meet your family, Shiver."

He raised a brow. "There isn't a kind, Losha. There's only you, and I want you to meet the duke and duchess."

"I'm not interested."

Shiver folded his arms. "Be honest with me. Tell me why you're so resistant."

"I've already told you. Again and again."

"The only thing you've said is that we don't have 'that' kind of relationship. Whatever 'that' means."

"It's shagging, Shiver. Enjoyable, but nonetheless, only shagging."

"I want more."

"You're a marquess."

"I am that."

"One day you'll be a duke."

"Perhaps, and perhaps not."

"And what about SIS?"

"You don't think SIS knows about us?"

I shivered. I did, and that was a big part of the problem, because if SIS knew, so did United Russia.

"Shiver…I can't…"

"You can."

"That isn't what I mean. What I'm trying to tell you is that I can't…have children."

Shiver Whittaker was trained not to react, yet I saw it when he did. Anyone else might have missed it, but I didn't. When I turned and walked away, he didn't stop me.

"I don't care," he said right before I closed the door to the bathroom. It was better that I didn't see his face when he said it; I wouldn't have been able to bear the lie.

***

Now, here I was, hiding the baby I told Shiver I couldn't have.

"He's beautiful," gasped Zary when she and Gunner walked in the house on the island a couple of days after Christmas.

"Would you like to hold him?" I asked.

"Could I?"

I laughed. "Of course you can." I waited while Gunner helped my dearest friend in the world with her coat, and when she sat down, I handed her the baby.

"I'm scared," Zary said before I let go.

"Of what?"

"I don't know…that I'll break him or something."

I caught Gunner's indulgent smile as he watched his fiancée hold my baby. Just a glimpse of how much he loved Zary convinced me they were going to make great parents. Not that I was an expert. Far from it, actually.

A nurse at the hospital where Kazmir was born had told me to listen to my heart when it came to my baby.

"Don't let anyone tell you that you're doing anything wrong or right. Follow your heart, you will be a perfect mother," she'd told me the day Kazmir and I checked out of the hospital.

I'd read countless books about pregnancy and motherhood, terrified of things like colic and not being able to breastfeed, but so far, Kazmir was happy and healthy. The traveling and disruption to his schedule had taken a minor toll, but now that we'd been on the island for three days, his routine and sleep patterns had evened out.

It wasn't as true for me though; I hadn't slept more than two or three hours each night.

"I'm sorry I couldn't get here sooner," said Zary, smiling at the baby.

"If you two don't need me, I'm going to walk the island."

Zary, enthralled with Kazmir, nodded but didn't answer.

"Thank you, Gunner," I said when he motioned for me to follow.

"You're welcome. Is everything okay with the house? Is there anything you need?"

"Everything is wonderful. Again, thank you."

Gunner nodded and walked out the front door.

"He loves you so much," I said after the door closed behind him.

"I never dreamed a life like this existed."

I hadn't either, although for a different reason. Soon, Zary would understand that too, when their baby was born.

When Kazmir got fussy, I took him from my friend's arms.

"What did I do wrong?" she asked.

"Nothing." I smiled. "He's just hungry." I motioned for Zary to follow me into the living room and then sat in one of the rocking chairs. Once the baby was settled on my breast, I closed my eyes momentarily, reminding myself to celebrate being a mother rather than spend time regretting that Kazmir's father wasn't in his life.

"Are you okay?" Zary asked.

"I am." I opened my eyes. "Tired, but that's to be expected."

"Gunner wanted me to tell you that you and Kazmir can stay here as long as you like."

"Isn't this your home?"

Zary shrugged. "I don't think we've necessarily figured that out yet."

"This place suits you," I said, looking around the rustic yet refined space.

"I have to admit, the bathroom is my favorite room in the house."

"The bathroom?"

"Don't tell me you haven't been in there. Where are you sleeping?"

The night Gunner brought Kazmir and me to the island, he'd told me that I was welcome to stay in the master bedroom, but I hadn't. Instead, the baby and I had been sleeping in the bedroom farthest from the front door, near the back of the house.

"You have to check it out. The bathtub alone…"

I smiled.

"What?"

"I love seeing you so happy."

"As I said before, I never would've dreamed. It seems only yesterday I was running for my life, not knowing who I could and couldn't trust. I couldn't find you…I'm sorry. I don't mean that any of it was your fault."

"I understand."

"Losha?"

"Mm-hmm?"

"The baby…is he Shiver's?"

I shook my head. "No, Zary. He isn't."

Whether Zary believed me didn't matter. Protecting Kazmir was my only priority, whether it be from United Russia or from the man who knew nothing about him.

"Tell me about the last few months of your life," said Zary after I put Kazmir in the crib for a nap.

I sighed. "I knew my departure from United Russia was inevitable, as did you. I'm sure you took many of the same precautions as I."

Zary nodded.

"I'd been stashing money long before I had any thoughts of leaving Russia and before I knew I was pregnant."

"Where did you go?"

"Sweden, Germany, and Switzerland. That's where Kazmir was born. And then to Finland."

"You must've been terrified."

"No more I suppose than I was most of my life. However, after my son was born, my outlook changed. I no longer looked at life as something I had to survive. Instead, it became something I wanted to live, and to share with my son, if I could keep him safe."

"I've told you again and again the bounty has been lifted."

"I know."

"But you don't trust it."

"I will never trust United Russia." I was tempted to say that I didn't have the same network of protection that Zary had, but my lack of it wasn't my friend's fault.

"Who is Kazmir's father, Losha?"

I stood, folded my arms, and looked out the window at the forest behind the house. I hated lying to Zary, but I would never divulge that information to anyone. The secret would stay with me until I died, after which, both Kazmir and his father would receive documentation that, in essence, would introduce them to one another.

Every day, I prayed that my death would be a long way off and that Kazmir would be a young man with a life of his own—perhaps even a family—by the time he was told his father's identity.

"I understand if you don't wish to say."

"I'm sorry, Zary."

When I mentioned that I intended to look for a more permanent place for Kazmir and me to live, both Zary and Gunner told me it wasn't necessary and that we'd discuss it further when they next visited.

"I'll call you," said Zary, kissing both me and Kazmir.

The house was too quiet after they left, at least when the baby was asleep. I'd always been a solitary person. What was it about being a mother that made me long for someone else to talk to—someone who could talk back?

Instead of taking the time to rest myself, my mind wandered to things I'd rather not remember. Usually it was Shiver, but today, I thought back to when Zary and I first met.

***

While I knew the KGB would only take teenagers, the fragile-looking blonde girl they'd just put in the van didn't look much over thirteen. I may not have even noticed her if, like the others, she was whining and weeping. Instead, the girl showed no emotion at all, just like me. I watched her, but the girl didn't look up once—not until we arrived at Lubyanka Square.

I stayed close to her as we were led through the halls of the KGB headquarters and to the dormitory-style rooms where we were paired up. I pushed my way through the remaining girls when I saw one of our escorts eyeing the blonde girl.

"You two," he barked in Russian, pointing first to us and then to the door.

Once inside with the door closed, the girl started to speak, but I shook my head. I took out the piece of paper and pencil I'd had hidden in the bottom of my shoe.

The room is bugged, I wrote.

The girl nodded.

Do you know sign language?

She shook her head.

***

As it turned out, the girl, Zaryana, and I were the same age and had both been orphaned under the age of ten. While we hadn't been in the same orphanage in Moscow, the conditions of where we'd lived were almost identical.

Zary had proven to be a quick study. Not only had she memorized the entire alphabet of sign language, we'd also worked on a few signals we could communicate with quickly. The first of which had been for "danger."

The training we underwent was rigorous, but we added more to it. As we progressed and rose in the initial ranks of the KGB, we'd been awarded more and more freedom. When we were allowed to leave Lubyanka Square, Zaryana and I would practice sparring, increase our aerobic endurance, and study the things the KGB hadn't yet taught us but we gleaned were coming.

I heard Kazmir's cries and hurried into the bedroom. Instead of the happy baby he usually was after waking from a nap, he looked flushed and was inconsolable. He felt warm to the touch, but that could be because he'd worked himself into such a frenzy.

Taking Kazmir into the bathroom, I pulled the thermometer out of the bag of baby things. When I saw it was over one hundred, I called Zary.

"I'm so sorry. I know you just left, but Kazmir is running a fever."

"We'll come right back," said Zary.

"You don't need to stay. Kazmir and I will be fine," I told Zary when she walked me into the hospital while Gunner parked the car.

"I'm not going anywhere. Besides, this is my fault."

"How is Kazmir having a fever your fault?"

"It didn't occur to me that the island wouldn't be an appropriate place for you to stay. I'm sorry, Losha. You would've been stuck there, and if anything worse…"

I couldn't allow myself to think about that. "I'm sorry. I need to speak with the nurse."

"Go ahead. Gunner and I will wait here."

"He's teething and running a low-grade fever. I'm so sorry to have called you back to the island. I'm so embarrassed," I told Zary over an hour later.

"Please don't be. Gunner and I have been discussing the…situation, and we've come up with an idea."

"We've been such an intrusion as it is."

"As I was saying, Gunner and Razor have a place on the West Coast, in California. Neither of them lives there full-time. So it would be perfect."

"Zary, I couldn't impose further."

"Actually, you'd be doing me a favor," said Gunner, walking into the emergency waiting room with his phone in his hand. "I may need to leave without much warning."

I caught the look that passed between Zary and her soon-to-be husband. Neither needed to explain what Gunner was referring to. Regardless of the specifics, I knew there was an op brewing.

"I would feel better if Zary wasn't alone. If you agree, we can leave tonight."

"Gunner will go to the island, get your things, and make arrangements to return your rental car."

I shook my head. *"Eto slishkom mnogo."*

Zary's eyes bored into mine. "It isn't too much. It would never be too much. If it weren't for you…" Zary's eyes filled with tears. "Please say you'll let us do this for you and Kazmir."

Did I really have a choice? I could be stubborn and refuse, but my pride would have negative ramifications for my baby. "Thank you."

"I'll get the car," said Gunner.

"He hasn't told anyone, Losha."

My grip on Zary's hand tightened. "If you're asking if he can, the answer is still no. No one can know about Kazmir."

"I understand."

"I'm making this too hard on you."

"We only need to know the boundaries. If you say no one can know, then no one will."

I cradled the sleeping Kazmir.

"May I hold him?"

"Of course," I said, gently shifting the baby into Zary's arms.

7

Shiver

"Hey, Shiv," said Doc when he answered my call.

"We've just landed at Reagan."

"I wish I had better news for you…"

"What's happened?"

"Losha isn't in Washington anymore."

"Bloody hell." I ran my hand through my hair. "Where is she?"

"I believe she's on her way to California."

"Why?"

"I can't answer that, and Shiv, this is starting to get a little tricky on my end."

"What do you mean?"

"I believe she may be traveling with Zary."

"Which means Gunner knows where she is."

"That's right."

"And he hasn't told you that directly."

"You're catching on."

I'd say I was surprised, but I wasn't. If there was anyone Losha would turn to for help, it would be Zary. I should've considered that possibility sooner.

"How do you want to move forward?" I asked.

"At this point, I'm handing it off to you."

"Understood. Send me the bill for time and expenses, Doc. I appreciate all you and the K19 crew have done, especially at this time of the year."

"By all means, Shiv, and good luck to you."

I disconnected the call when I saw Darrow come out of the ladies' room.

"Ready?" she asked.

"There's been a slight change of plans."

"What now?"

"I have to leave tonight, once you're settled in at the hotel."

Darrow rolled her eyes. "So you're dumping me off, is that right?"

"Hardly, sweet pea. I'm not leaving right away. I just told you that I won't leave until you're settled."

"And I told you that my friend won't be back until tomorrow."

I sighed. "Tell me again who you're here to visit?"

"I've told you countless times. Poppy and I were at university together. Her father is Bryce Davies."

"Right." Now I remembered. Davies and the duke had never gotten on well, so Darrow had spent more time at their place than Poppy had at Whittaker Abbey. "I thought you were meeting friends, not a friend."

Darrow rolled her eyes. "You're my brother, not the duke. Give it a rest, Thornton."

It was a fine line I walked between being her older brother, as she said, and an MI6 agent. "Fancy a pint before we catch a taxi?"

"I thought you'd never ask."

I directed Darrow toward the USO lounge and, when we walked inside, saw someone who looked familiar.

"Alegria?"

"Shiver?" She kissed me on both cheeks.

"This is my sister, Darrow. Darrow, meet Alegria. She's with K19."

"It's nice to meet you." Darrow looked from Alegria to me. "Do you ever go anywhere without running into someone you know?"

"Rarely."

"Where are you headed?" Alegria asked.

"My brother is dropping me off to stay with friends in DC. Where he's going is always a mystery."

"Why are you here?" I asked.

"Dutch and Mantis are flying in from Mogadishu."

I raised a brow. From what I'd heard, Alegria had ended a long-term relationship with Mantis and had recently started seeing Dutch. What complicated things further was that Dutch and Mantis had been best friends since they both attended the Air Force Academy in Colorado.

"Don't ask," she said, looking away and then pulling out her phone when it vibrated. "They've landed."

"Tell them we're here," I suggested, not knowing what else to say.

"Do you have plans? Maybe we could all have dinner? My friends won't be back until tomorrow, but my brother couldn't wait another day to dump me here."

"It isn't like that," I muttered, wishing my sister hadn't suggested dinner. As it was, I would be hard-pressed to find a flight to the West Coast tonight.

Two hours later, I was about to give up hope that dinner would ever come to an end.

"Excuse me," I heard Darrow say, and watched her walk in the direction of the ladies' room.

"Anything I can help with?" Mantis asked when Dutch and Alegria went off to have what appeared to be a private conversation.

"Thanks, but I don't think so."

Mantis nodded. "Let me know if you change your mind."

I nodded in return. "What about you?"

"Come again?"

"Anything I can help with?"

Mantis looked over his shoulder at Dutch and Alegria, whose discussion appeared to have turned heated. "I don't think there's much hope."

I shook my head. "You're wrong."

"What makes you think so?"

"After watching the two of you tonight, it's obvious Alegria still loves you."

"What if that isn't enough?"

"I've wondered that myself, mate." I had no idea what compelled me to say that out loud, but there it was. I was relieved when Mantis didn't ask what I meant.

"Hey, Shiv."

"Pinch? You don't sound well."

"Long day. Listen, I have an update on Kuznetsov's whereabouts."

"I talked to Doc earlier."

"And?"

"I'm headed to the West Coast in the morning. I'll take it from here, Pinch. There's something else I need your help with though."

"Name it."

"Darrow is meeting up with Poppy Davies here in DC; however, she's being vague about who else she's spending time with."

"I'll see what I can find out."

"Thanks, mate. As with Losha, this is personal. Send me the bill for your time and expenses."

While Darrow stayed closer to the capital, I went back across the Potomac and got a room near the airport. I was scheduled on the first flight out in the morning and needed to get some rest.

I poured a glass of scotch and sat near the window from where I could see the lights shining on the river.

How in the hell had I gotten here? How had something I was so certain of, turned into such a Charlie Foxtrot?

One day I was in bed with Losha's luscious body next to mine, having breakfast, and trying to convince her again to come to Bedfordshire and meet my family. The next, I was chasing her around the globe for the sole purpose of finding out who the wanker was that she'd left me for.

I downed what was in the glass, thought about having another, but stretched out on the bed instead and fell asleep without as much as taking my shoes off.

8

Losha

"This is my first time here too," Zary told me while we waited for the electronic gate to open. "Gunner spoke with Razor, who owns the other half of the duplex; he and his wife are on their way to their home in Oregon."

I looked out of the window when Gunner drove through the gate, and shook my head. Every time Zary said she'd never dreamed she'd live a life like the one she was living, I understood what she meant more.

"It's so beautiful." I'd almost added that I didn't know how I'd ever repay their kindness and generosity, but I'd already said it so often I felt as though it was beginning to sound meaningless.

When Gunner parked and I got out of the car, I saw that a lush Japanese garden surrounded what looked like two connected structures with koi ponds in front of each. The exterior of the houses was dark wood with a clay roof, and from where I stood, I could see the ocean.

"Is that a beach?" I asked.

"It is." Gunner smiled. "Although the Pacific Ocean doesn't get very warm even in the summer. In the winter, it is downright freezing."

I was too ashamed to admit I'd never learned to swim, so getting into the water would've been out of the question no matter how warm it got.

"We'll set you up over here." Gunner led me to the front door of the house on the right. "The duplex is connected only by the garages. There's no direct access between the two, so you're assured plenty of privacy."

"Thank you," I said for what felt like the millionth time.

"I'll bring everything inside while you and Zary check the place out."

After we'd landed at the airport in San Luis Obispo, we stopped at a large department store where Zary and Gunner filled carts with everything a baby could possibly require.

"We'll need it soon enough," Zary had said. "You can use it until we do."

They'd bought a car seat, a regular-size crib, a changing table, and a chair called a glider that came with an ottoman and moved back and forth, similar to a rocking chair, but looked far more comfortable.

There was bedding, a tiny bathtub, blankets, diapers, and so many clothes that I doubted Kazmir would have time to wear them all before he was too big for them to fit.

"Whatever else we need, we can shop for later," Zary had told me when we got ready to check out.

When I'd tried to pay for the purchases, Gunner put his hand on mine.

"Let us do this," he'd said barely above a whisper, making my eyes fill with tears for the countless time.

"Gunner will set everything up tomorrow if that's okay."

I smiled. "I can do it."

"I know," my friend said, walking over to kiss Kazmir's cheek. "I just don't know how you ever put him down."

"Would you like to hold him?"

I chuckled when Zary clapped her hands. "I always want to hold him."

"I'll help Gunner bring things inside."

"You can offer, but he won't let you."

"Why not?"

"Maybe the lighter things, but not if something's heavy."

I put my hands on my hips. "You're kidding."

"I'm not. And whatever you do, don't ever open a door for yourself when he's around."

"Wow."

"I know. It's just how he is."

"He does know what you used to do for a living, right?"

Zary giggled. "We go to the shooting range, and we train together; it's just the gentlemanly stuff he gets weird about."

"There's nothing weird about being a gentleman," said Gunner, coming in with the box the crib was in. "I put an order in for dinner if that's okay with both of you." He looked at his watch. "It should be here in about an hour."

I would've offered to cook, but other than heating things up, I wasn't very good at it. I wondered if Zary was.

"I'll let you get some rest," said Zary when we finished cleaning up from our take-out dinner.

I kissed both of Zary's cheeks and murmured my thanks. "Please tell Gunner I said thank you and good night."

He'd left a few minutes ago, saying he had a call to make. I guessed that it had something to do with the op that he believed he'd be summoned for in the not-too-distant future.

"I'll see you in the morning, and, Losha, please try to get some rest."

Tonight I felt tired enough that I might just be able to get a full night's sleep. The books I'd read about what to expect with an infant talked a lot about trying to get a baby to sleep through the night. Kazmir didn't seem to have as much difficulty with it as I did.

I stretched my arms above my head and looked around the room for a clock. It had to be at least seven, but Kazmir was still asleep in the portable crib set up next to the bed.

Resting my head back against the pillows, I listened to the sound of waves crashing against the shore that had lulled me to a much-needed restful sleep last night.

I'd protested all that Zary and Gunner were doing for me countless times, but I had to admit, this morning

I was grateful they'd insisted. I hadn't felt so relaxed in as long as I could remember.

Rolling over in the bed to look out at the ocean, I tried to think back to a time when I'd felt such a sense of peace and calm in my life. Unfortunately, the memory I came up with, filled me with the same angst that kept me awake most nights.

Shiver. The last time I'd felt this relaxed was when I was with him. Before we'd argued and I'd threatened to leave, but he hadn't let me.

***

When I came out of the bathroom, Shiver was sitting in a chair by the bed. He was shirtless, but he'd put his trousers on.

"Come here," he said, holding his hand out.

"Shiv…"

"Please."

I walked closer and let him pull me onto his lap.

He nuzzled my neck. "I don't care whether you're able to have a baby or not."

"I don't believe you."

"I'm not lying to you, Losha. It's you I love. Whatever life brings or doesn't, as long as we're together, we'll make it work."

When I tried to move away, Shiver held me tighter.

"We aren't together. We don't share a life. Every few months, we share a bed."

Shiver ran his finger from my chin, down my neck, and into the opening of my robe. "I'll do whatever it takes, Losha. Say the word, and I'll help you leave UR."

"It isn't that simple, and you know it." I sighed when his lips followed the same trail his finger had.

He stood, carried me back to the bed, untied the robe's sash, and spread it open.

"Lie back and let me look at you. Give me something to dream about when I close my eyes and you aren't beside me."

Shiver unfastened his trousers, then slid them off his hips and onto the floor.

I wanted the same thing—a memory of him naked, standing above me, his eyes heated, and his body rock hard.

As much as I loved him, I'd never been able to tell him so—even now.

He rested above me and looked into my eyes. "Why do I feel as though you're about to say goodbye to me forever?"

I turned my head when my eyes filled with tears, but he grasped my chin.

"Look at me," he said, waiting until I opened my eyes to continue. "I'm not going to let you do this."

"What makes you think you have a choice?"

"If you walk away, I'll come after you. If you hide from me, I'll find you. I'm never letting you go, Losha. That's a promise I intend to keep for the rest of my life."

***

Would he keep that promise? Was he looking for me now? If he found me, what would he say when he discovered I'd had his baby and hadn't intended to ever tell him? Would he try to take Kazmir from me? Would he want to raise the baby himself in the bosom of his noble family back in England?

There could only be one thing that hurt as much as not having Shiver in my life, and that would be losing my son. I'd never let that happen. If he found us, I would have to run again, somewhere farther, go deeper, until he finally gave up and let me live my life without him in it.

When I looked over, my baby boy's eyes were wide open, and he was staring at me with a look on his cherubic face so sweet, it was as though he could read my thoughts.

Kazmir raised his hands, and I crawled over to pick him up.

"Good morning, my precious boy."

Kazmir cooed and latched on to my breast. As he nursed, I ran my fingers through his wavy hair that was more like Shiver's than mine.

"I love you, my Kazmir, and I'll never, ever let your father take you away from me."

I took a bath in the big jetted tub that looked out over the ocean, holding Kazmir in my arms while he played in the water.

Later, I went into the kitchen to look for something to eat. Kazmir was getting old enough that soon he would want more than my milk for nourishment. Maybe now would be a good time for me to learn to cook. I should be able to handle simple things, like scrambled eggs, without making too much of a mess of them.

I carried the portable crib from the bedroom to the kitchen and set Kazmir in it. He babbled and hugged the stuffed animals I had put in with him. Once I finished breakfast, I'd look for the high chair Gunner and

Zary had purchased the night before, and put it together so Kazmir could sit and watch me cook.

I found a pan and got the eggs out of the refrigerator. I rested my hands against the counter as my mind was flooded with a rare memory from my childhood.

My mother was in a kitchen a fraction of the size of this one, taking a pan out of the oven instead of a cupboard. Space had been tight, I remembered. Eggs sat in a bowl on the counter.

The ties of an apron wrapped around the woman's thick waist, and her long hair, sprinkled with gray, hung down her back. I closed my eyes, willing the woman to turn around in my memory so I could see her face, but hard as I tried to recall that simple detail, it wouldn't come. How old had I been? I couldn't remember that detail either. There was a rap on the front door.

"Good, you're awake," said Zary, letting herself in. She stood by the portable crib that did double duty as a playpen. "May I?"

"You never have to ask."

Zary didn't just smile; she beamed, reminding me again that, as happy as I was for her, I couldn't tamp down the envy I so often felt.

"There's so much for us to catch up on." Zary laughed as she playfully nipped at Kazmir's hands.

"Is there?"

"I don't know how much you heard while you were underground."

"How would I have heard anything?" I snapped.

"I'm sorry. I didn't mean to upset you."

I closed my eyes and looked up at the ceiling, wishing I hadn't been so abrupt with the woman who had been nothing but loving toward me. "I'm the one who's sorry. Please, tell me what's been happening."

An hour later, when Zary finished the tale of how she'd discovered her long-since-believed-dead father was alive, as was her mother, my mind was reeling.

"You have a half sister too?"

"Two actually," Zary answered. "They're twins. In fact, Ava is Razor's wife."

I knew that should mean something to me, but with everything Zary had just told me, I couldn't piece it all together.

"Razor is Gunner's friend. He owns this side of the duplex," Zary explained, perhaps picking up on my confusion.

"Right. I knew the name sounded familiar." Razor knew that Gunner and Zary had brought me here; did he also know about my baby?

"What's wrong?" Zary asked.

"Nothing. It's just a lot to take in."

"It's more to live through."

"Yes," I said.

"Are you okay?"

I wished I could describe the pressure of being alone in the world that had settled on my chest. Not only did Zary have Gunner; she had an entire family.

There wouldn't be any parents discovered alive for me. I was there the day my mother had died, just like the day my father had. It was more than a year apart and many years ago, but the horribly graphic memories of their deaths still haunted me.

"Perhaps I shouldn't have told you."

"It isn't that. I'm so happy for you, Zary. I mean that sincerely."

"But?"

"I wish I could explain, but I can't." I'd never been the kind of person who found pleasure in another person's unhappiness, not that I'd experienced the empathy that would make me feel one way or another

very often. My life had been limited to only two relationships. The one with Zary had been born out of our
shared misfortune, and the one with Shiver I'd always
considered temporary. There wasn't anyone else. Not
until Kazmir.

"Gunner said the town of Cambria is lovely. There
are shops and restaurants that line the main street, and
today is predicted to be relatively warm for January."

"A walk sounds quite nice."

"Where is the box with the pram in it?" Zary asked.

I pointed to the hallway. "I think Gunner put everything in there."

Zary looked at the stove. "Were you cooking?"

"Just eggs."

"Can I help?"

I laughed out loud. Sometimes the best thing about
my friendship with Zary was that neither of us had
anything resembling a normal life. Zary understood
innately that I wouldn't know how to cook eggs
without help.

9

Shiver

I walked off the plane and through the terminal of the small airport, trying to decide whether to contact Gunner or just show up at the house. I understood Doc's dilemma in the same way I would've if someone I worked with wasn't being completely forthcoming with me.

Gunner and Razor owned property in the seaside village of Cambria, and if Losha was with him and Zary, it made perfect sense that this would be where he'd brought her.

I picked up the rental car I'd reserved and drove north, easily finding the walled and gated property I'd visited less than a handful of times. I stopped far enough away that I wouldn't be spotted, mulling over how to proceed.

Before I came to a decision, I saw the gate open and a car pull out onto the road. When it went in the opposite direction of where I was parked, I followed.

The car turned a corner and slowed. From where I was, I could see Zary was driving and Losha was in the front passenger seat.

They stopped and she got out of the car, giving me a better look. If it were possible, she looked more beautiful than she ever had. She was dressed in jeans and a bulky sweater, and her long dark hair swayed in waves down her back.

I watched Losha open the rear passenger door while Zary got something out of the trunk. I held my breath when she leaned into the car. When she straightened up, she was holding a baby bundled in blankets in her arms. Losha brought her lips to the child's cheek. I was at once moved and sickened. She was a picture-perfect loving mother of a baby she'd made with another man.

Zary opened a pram, and Losha leaned down to fasten the baby in it. From where I sat in the car, I couldn't see her expression, but it was as though an aura of love and warmth surrounded her.

Never once had I seen her look at anyone or anything with such unabashed affection. It made my heart ache even though it was love for a child rather than another man.

But how could she not love someone with whom she'd created another life? My chest filled with unimaginable pain, knowing she must.

I got out of the car when the women had walked far enough away in the opposite direction, and followed them as they rounded the corner onto the main street of the town.

Whenever they ducked into a shop, I stopped and pretended to be looking at my phone like so many others walking down the street. I kept myself prepared for them to come in my direction, scoping out where I might find cover if they did, but so far they hadn't.

Every once in a while, her laugh would waft through the air and settle on me like a warm woolen. I so missed the sound of it. If only I could walk up and greet her as an old friend might. Cup her cheek with my palm and bring a chaste kiss to her lips. If only I could just feel her near me.

10

Losha

"Shall we stop for lunch?" Zary asked when we came out of a shop.

"Good idea. Kazmir is restless." I turned my head, looking back from where we'd come, and my heart stopped. There, not twenty yards from me, stood the person I loved and feared equally. "Shiver," I whispered.

He was here, watching me for God knew how long. As we walked toward one another, I looked for animosity in his eyes, but didn't see it. Instead, they were full of love and longing.

"Losha," he murmured when we were close enough that he could reach out and touch the side of my face with his finger. "How I've missed you."

I wanted nothing more than to fall into his embrace, tell him I'd missed him too, and feel his lips on mine. Instead, I took a step back.

"What are you doing here, Shiver?"

"I would think that's obvious."

I raised a brow in a feeble attempt to pretend it wasn't.

"I have so many questions," he said, looking behind me to where Zary stood with Kazmir.

I wished I could lie and tell him the baby was Zary's rather than mine, but it was too late for that.

"He's beautiful, Losha. What's his name?"

"Kazmir," I whispered, suddenly overcome by an urge to shout at him to stay away from my baby as his eyes remained riveted on him.

Slowly, I turned, wanting to see what he saw. Did he remind him of anyone? Did Kazmir look like he had as a baby? I had no photos of myself as an infant to know if he resembled me.

"Shiver, I…"

His gaze rested back on me. He studied my face as he waited for me to continue. When I didn't, he drew in a deep breath. "Is there somewhere we can talk?"

I looked to Zary.

"I can take Kazmir back to the house if you'd like," she offered.

"No," I said, not wanting my son out of my sight. "We'll all go back to the house."

Shiver nodded. "Wherever you'd be most comfortable."

"Are you okay?" Zary asked when we returned to the car.

"I'm not sure yet."

"Are you happy to see him?"

Was I? It was impossible to say. Too many emotions warred within me. As much as I longed to wrap my arms around him and never let go, I equally wanted to push him away and tell him never to contact me again.

"Losha, I—"

"I'm not ready to talk about it, Zary."

"I just want you to know that neither Gunner nor I told Shiver you were here."

"No? At least one of you must have told someone."

I watched as my friend's eyes grew dark. "I didn't and neither did he. I am sorry he found you, though."

"Don't be." I buckled Kazmir into the car seat and opened the front passenger door. "Listen. I'm not angry. This was inevitable."

Zary nodded and started the engine. "I just have one thing to say, Losha. Kazmir resembles him."

I'd seen it too. When I'd looked from his face to my son's, it was as plain as day. My baby was the spitting image of his father.

11

Shiver

Fear, longing, regret, and hunger all rowed within me. I took several deep breaths in an attempt to settle my racing heart. Just being in Losha's presence again flooded my system with adrenaline.

The baby looked so much like her that I yearned to just sit and stare at him. There had been a point in time when I wondered what she'd looked like as a child. Now I knew, at least as a baby.

Kazmir. That's what she'd named him. When she said it, I could feel the pride and love that poured out of her. There was no question the baby was Losha's. But who was the father? Would she tell me if I asked, or would she refuse, saying it was none of my business?

When we arrived at the house, I waited behind them for the gate to open and then followed them inside the compound.

Gunner came out of one of the front doors and walked over to the car. "Shiver."

"It's good to see you." We embraced, patting each other on the back.

"Listen—"

"It's okay, Gunner. I understand."

"I'm relieved to hear it."

I watched Losha get the baby out of the car seat. "Can I help?"

"Do you want me to take him?" Zary asked.

Losha shook her head. "We'll be fine."

"What can I do?" I asked when Zary and Gunner walked to the door I'd seen him come out of.

"The house code is 1223," she said, motioning to the keypad.

"Got it." I opened the door when the lock clicked and held it for her. "Do you need anything from the car?"

"Not for now," Losha said, shifting the baby to her other hip. "He's hungry."

I nodded.

"Will it make you uncomfortable?"

"What's that?"

"If I feed him."

I shook my head, wondering why she thought it might. When she sat and unfastened the buttons on her shirt, I understood, watching in fascination as the baby found his mother's breast. When his tiny hand rested near Losha's face, I felt certain it was the most beautiful thing I'd ever seen.

I looked up and found her studying me in the same way I'd been studying her baby.

"Thank you."

"What for?"

"Letting me…in." I was so emotionally overcome, I couldn't think of the right words to describe the way I was feeling. "I never…"

"What, Shiver? You never what?"

I ran my hand through my hair, glancing back at the baby. "Dreamed that anything so beautiful existed."

"I know," she whispered. "He takes my breath away."

"Not just him. Both of you. I'm so in awe I can hardly speak."

Losha's eyes filled with tears, and she turned her head away. "I'm sorry," she whispered.

"What for, Losha? Why are you sorry?"

"So many things."

I looked out at the ocean. "Me too. So many things." In that moment, I was consumed by regret. Why couldn't this have been something we'd done together? Why had she shared this miracle with someone other than me? I wanted to shout the questions at her, while at the same time, never wanting to know the answers.

"Can you ever forgive me?" I thought I heard her say.

"What ever for?"

She shrugged, her eyes resting on her baby.

"I would never begrudge you this happiness, Losha. Not ever. It's so obvious that you were meant to be a mother. I would never dream of wishing anything else for you or him."

"But…"

"Who is he, Losha?"

"What do you mean?"

"Who is the man you loved enough to have a child with? Who is the man you loved in a way you could never love me?"

12

Losha

The tears in Shiver's eyes broke my heart. Did he really not know? How could he not realize Kazmir was his son? Couldn't he see the resemblance?

God, I didn't know what to do. Should I tell him, or let him believe the lie he'd just spoken?

"Are you with him?"

I shook my head. "No."

"Do you love him?"

"With all my heart."

Shiver closed his eyes and rested his head against the back of the chair. Pain etched his beautiful face. Why couldn't I bring myself to take his hurt away? Why had it always been impossible to tell him how I felt, that I did love him?

In the same way I'd never been able to bring myself to say the words he wanted to hear, I couldn't bring myself to tell him Kazmir was his.

He looked into my eyes. "I should go."

"Already?"

"I thought you'd want me to."

"No." I wished I was strong enough to let him leave, but I wasn't. "Would you stay? A little while longer?"

"Of course. Is there anything I can do to help?" he asked, eyeing the boxes sitting in the hall.

I shifted Kazmir to the opposite breast. "Can you assemble furniture?"

"I am an MI6 agent, Losha."

I laughed. "Does that mean you're qualified to put a crib together?"

"It means I'm a bloody superhero, woman."

I loved the playfulness in his voice. This was the Shiver I loved with all my heart and soul, the man who could make me laugh no matter the conflict I faced.

An hour later, we'd not only assembled the crib, we'd also put together the changing table and the high chair. All that was left was the glider, which wouldn't take long.

"Where does this all go?" he asked.

"I haven't figured that out yet."

Shiver stood. "Bedroom's that way?" he asked.

"Yes."

"Wow," I heard him gasp when he entered the master. "Quite a view."

Kazmir held out his arms to be picked up, and I carried him into where Shiver was still marveling at the expanse of ocean visible through the window.

When I stood next to him, the baby fussed, trying to squirm out of my arms. "Sorry. He wants you."

Shiver held out a finger which Kazmir grabbed with his tiny hand. "He looks so much like you."

"Do you think so?"

"You don't?" He held out his arms, and the baby scrambled into them. "Look," he said. "He's your mirror image."

I didn't agree. To me, he looked just like Shiver. I watched as Kazmir snuggled into him and he bent his neck to kiss his forehead.

"He's getting tired," I told him. "Would you like to nap in your new crib?"

Kazmir buried his face in Shiver's chest.

"It's the n-word. He doesn't like naps," I added when he looked confused.

"I can hold him a bit longer. If it's okay with you."

"Of course it is." I walked out of the bedroom, and Shiver followed. I pointed to the chair I'd been sitting in when I fed him. "If you rock him, he'll doze off."

13

Shiver

In the span of a few minutes, I'd hopelessly, completely, absolutely fallen head-over-heels in love with the baby I held in my arms. It didn't matter who Kazmir's biological father was, I felt a propriety so intense that I knew I'd protect the little boy with every fiber of my being, even my life.

Never before had I felt a love like this. The strength of it was equal to the love I felt for Losha, but at the same time, it felt so different. I never wanted to let the baby go, even to sleep. I wanted to hold Kazmir in my arms, day and night, night and day.

How Losha ever let him go, I couldn't fathom. I closed my eyes and breathed in the sweetest scent I'd ever known.

"Good nap?" Losha asked from the kitchen.

"What's that?"

She pointed at the clock hanging on the wall. "You've been asleep for more than an hour."

Had I been? *Jesus.* "Sorry, I…uh…haven't been sleeping well."

"Don't apologize," she whispered, coming closer and stroking the baby's hair. "He looks as though he's having pleasant dreams. As did you."

I bent my neck but couldn't see the baby's face. However, Losha was right about my dreams. I'd fallen asleep imagining that this was our life. A home by the sea, the two of us together with the baby; it felt sublime.

It wasn't that simple, though. There was the question of who Kazmir's father was, and while Losha said they weren't together, she'd also said she loved him. I closed my eyes against the pain, wishing that if I asked, she'd answer honestly and tell me who he was.

"He's getting sweaty," she said, plucking the baby from my arms that with the loss, felt painfully empty. "I'll put him down and come back."

I stood to follow, but stopped when I heard Losha singing. It felt too intimate of a moment to intrude on, so I stood outside the door. I didn't recognize the tune, only that it sounded like a Russian lullaby. Was it something she remembered from her childhood?

I moved aside when she came out, closing the door behind her. "He'll sleep for another hour, at least."

That would give us time to talk, but I was hesitant to begin a conversation that would make us both so uncomfortable.

"How's your family?" she asked.

"My father had a stroke," I began. "He had several, in fact."

"I'm sorry to hear. Is he recovering well?"

I shook my head. "He isn't recovering at all."

"Oh, Shiv. I'm sorry. I don't know what else to say."

I ran my hand through my hair and pointed to the deck outside. "Think it's warm enough to sit out there for a bit?"

Losha opened the slider and pulled a chair back from the table. I sat in the one beside her.

"He can't speak or eat. I'm not sure how much he's aware of. We talk to him as though he hears us. The duchess insists we do things like read the morning news to him, or sit with him while we have tea. There are times the tragedy of it feels unbearable."

"I wish I'd met him."

I looked at her; she was looking at the ocean. "I wish you had too."

"What do the doctors say?"

"Not much. To keep doing what we're doing, but not expect his condition to improve significantly."

She covered my hand with hers. I felt the simple touch throughout my body, and more than anything, I wanted to hold every inch of her against me. Instead, I closed my eyes, willing her not to pull away when I weaved my fingers with hers.

"Sweet Losha," I whispered. "You have always soothed me so."

"And you, me," she whispered too, as though by speaking quietly no one could hear the words we shouldn't be saying.

"I…God, I'm at such a loss."

"Me as well."

"Really?" I turned my body so it faced hers. "There are so many things I want to say, and at the same time, I want to hold you close to me and not utter a word."

Losha pulled her hand from mine and stood. "Come, Shiver," she said, walking back inside the house.

"Do you want me to leave?" I asked when she turned in the direction of the front door.

"No. I want you to come with me."

I followed her into the bedroom and toed off my shoes when I saw her do the same. When she lay down on the bed, I stretched my body next to hers.

"Hold me, Shiver," she pleaded.

I drew her into my arms. "Always." I closed my eyes and breathed in her scent. It was so different from Kazmir's, yet it filled me with a similar sense of peaceful longing.

I wished I could tell her how much I still loved her, that I'd do anything for her and her baby, but none of that could be said until I knew what Losha's relationship with Kazmir's father was.

She turned her body so she faced me. "Shiver, look at me."

I took a deep breath. "Do you have any idea what effect your body next to mine is having on me?" I asked.

"I do."

"Losha, please."

"Please what, Shiver?"

She brought her lips to mine, and I didn't hesitate. Her fervor matched mine when my tongue pushed inside her mouth and my fingers unfastened the buttons on her blouse. Once I had it open, I kissed my way from her mouth to her breasts. Losha unfastened the snap on her bra that released the cup.

"Handy." I circled her chafed nipple with my tongue. "Does this hurt?"

"A little," she confessed.

I brought my lips back to her mouth and pulled her body flush with mine. I kneaded the flesh of her behind with my fingers, bringing her sex in line with my hardness.

When she put her hands on the belt of my trousers, I stopped her. "Wait," I said, pulling back. "We shouldn't be doing this."

Losha sighed and tried to unfasten my belt.

"Don't." I moved her hands away.

"Shiver, please?"

I got off of the bed and stood, looking up at the ceiling and cursing whomever the stupid bastard was that stole her heart. "I can't do this." In anguish, I straightened my clothes, walked out of the bedroom, and out the front door.

"You won't be able to get out of the gate without the code," I heard Gunner say when I was about to open the door of the rental car. I didn't turn around. There would be no way for me to mask my heartache.

I'd allowed myself to fantasize what a life with Orina and Kazmir might be like. As soon as the reality hit of what we were about to do, I remembered she had told me, without any hesitation, that she was in love with another man.

"Shiv? You okay?" Gunner asked.

"I don't think I am," I said, turning around.

"Anything I can do?"

I shook my head. "Find the bastard that got her pregnant," I muttered.

"What did you say?"

"Sorry. That was inappropriate."

"Aren't you the baby's father?"

"Negative."

"You sure?"

"Yes, Gunner." I sighed and looked him in the eye.

Gunner rubbed the back of his neck. "I was certain you were."

"I'm not. Losha told me herself."

"What did she say?"

"I asked if she was still with the father of her baby, and she said she wasn't."

"Could apply to you," Gunner mumbled.

"I asked if she loved him."

"What was her response?"

"With all her heart."

My friend didn't say anything else, but his gaze remained focused on mine.

"What?"

"Did you ask who he was?"

"Of course I bloody asked who he was. Jesus, Gunner. This is hard enough without having to answer to you."

"I'm sorry, Shiv. It's just that…"

"For God's sake! *What?*"

"The baby looks just like you."

"That's utter nonsense. He looks like Losha."

"Zary saw it too, Shiv. She told me so when you came back from town."

"She's imagining it."

"I don't think so."

"I can't be the baby's father."

"You're sure?"

I counted back to the last time Losha and I were together. "How old is the baby?"

Gunner shrugged. "I figured you'd know."

"We used protection."

"And in the history of the universe, protection has never failed."

I glared at him. "This may be hysterical to you, mate, but it's my life we're talking about. Losha…" I took a deep breath, praying I wouldn't cry in front of my friend. "I thought…"

"Ask her. Be direct. 'Am I Kazmir's father?'" Gunner said, putting his hand on my shoulder.

"I need some time."

"Understood."

"Gunner, I…if she leaves…"

"I'll let you know."

"I know I'm putting you in a spot."

He shook his head. "You're not."

"Thanks, mate." I opened the car door.

"The same code works to get in," Gunner said, handing me a card.

I nodded and drove out the gate. I hadn't thought far enough ahead to make a plan for what I'd do next. I'd anticipated Losha telling me who Kazmir's father was, breaking my heart, and then I'd leave and never see her again. Instead, I didn't know what to think.

First, I'd fallen in love with her baby boy. Second, if I hadn't called a halt, we would've made love. We likely still would be. How was it possible for her to have sex with me if she loved another man "with all her heart"? I didn't believe she could have.

I drove to Moonstone Beach where several inns dotted the shoreline. Most had vacancy signs, so I pulled into the one that looked the least romantic. I hardly needed to come face-to-face with happy lovers.

I'd just closed the door of the hotel room behind me when my mobile vibrated. I hesitated, praying it was Losha calling to ask me to come back. Instead, I saw the call was from Wilder.

"Hey, Wild—"

"Shiver, the duke has slipped into a coma. You need to come home straightaway."

"*Jesus.* I'm sorry I left you to deal with all this, Sutton. I'll be on the next flight."

"You didn't leave me to deal with anything. I'm his son too."

"I know, I didn't mean—"

"Do you know where Darrow is?"

"At the Hay-Adams in DC."

"She isn't there. When I couldn't reach her by mobile, I called the hotel, and they told me she'd already checked out."

"I'll ring her when we hang up."

"Thanks, Shiv."

"How's the duchess?"

"Not well."

When my conversation with Wilder ended, I didn't ring Darrow; I called Pinch.

"Before you say anything," I began, "the duke is in a coma, and I need to make arrangements for Darrow to get back to England as soon as possible."

"I'll handle it, Shiv. We'll be on the next flight out."

I ended the call, not allowing myself to speculate on why Pinch could say definitively that they'd be on the next flight. As long as he got Darrow back to London immediately, I didn't need to know the details.

I looked around the room; there hadn't been time for me to unpack.

How I wished I hadn't received the call from Wilder, that my father's condition hadn't worsened, and that I didn't have to leave.

Foolish as it might be for me to consider what Gunner had said was a possibility, I also wished I had time to see Losha once more before I flew back to England, but I didn't.

I'd been able to book a commuter flight to Los Angeles that would give me barely enough time to catch the British Airways flight to Heathrow. For that to work, I needed to leave now.

14

Losha

"Losha? Are you here?" Zary shouted from the front door.

"Back here." I wiped away my tears and came out of the bedroom.

"I was worried…"

"You saw Shiver leave."

"Gunner did. They talked."

"Oh, dear."

"Is he gone? Gunner didn't say."

"I believe so." I tried not to cry, but I couldn't stop myself. "Oh, Zary, what have I done?"

She pulled me over to the sofa and put her arm around me. "Why didn't you tell him?"

Could I admit it out loud? Obviously, Zary didn't believe my lie about Shiver not being the baby's father.

"I don't know."

"Is he Kazmir's father?"

I hadn't told a single soul. This would be the first time I spoke the words I was so afraid to say.

"He is."

"Why don't you want him to know?"

"I have no answer."

"It's obvious you love each other."

"I've never told him that either."

"The man is a spy, Losha. Don't you think he's figured it out by now?"

I smiled. "Maybe when feelings are too close, it's harder to see."

"Mmm. Makes sense."

"Do you think he knows about Kazmir? He didn't act like he did."

"No. Definitely not."

"How can you be certain?"

"He and Gunner talked about it."

"What?" I gasped. "What did Gunner tell him?"

"Nothing. Gunner only guessed. Kazmir does look like him."

"We talked about it too. Shiver said he thinks he looks like me."

"Both of you."

"I see more of Shiver in him than me."

Zary smiled. "What are you going to do, Losha?"

"I have no idea."

"Can I make a suggestion?"

"Of course."

"Let Gunner and me watch Kazmir tonight. Call Shiver and ask him to come back. Talk it out. Tell him the truth about everything."

"I'm not sure I'm ready."

"Force yourself."

"He's still napping."

"Call me when he wakes up, and I'll come over and get him."

"Thank you, Zary."

"You'd do the same for me."

My phone sat on the table beside me. All I had to do was reach over, pick it up, and call him. Why was that so difficult?

I stood and paced near the windows, watching the sun go down on a day I hadn't dreamed would come this soon.

In a few minutes, Kazmir would be awake, and I'd have to feed him before Zary came over. If I didn't call Shiver now, it would be harder once the baby woke. I picked up the phone and pressed the code I'd put in my phone for him—*love.*

"Shiver?" I said when the phone stopped ringing but I didn't hear anything.

"Yes. Losha?"

"Is everything okay? You sound—"

"It's not, I'm afraid. My father has fallen into a coma. I'm on my way to the airport now."

"I'm so sorry. I'll let you go."

"Wait. Tell me why you called, Losha."

"I wanted to apologize for earlier. I had no right…"

"I see." He sighed. "Was there anything else?"

"No, that was all." I ended the call. The universe had made the decision for me. He was here only a short while, and now he had to leave for who knew how long. It wasn't the right time to tell him about his son, or how much I loved him and always would.

"Are you ready for me to come and get Kazmir?" Zary asked when I called.

"No. It won't be necessary."

"Why? What happened?"

"Shiver's father is in a coma. He had to return to England immediately."

"Oh, Losha, I'm so sorry."

"It's for the best."

"Hang on. In fact, I'll call you back."

I looked at the phone when the call ended. That was odd. Seconds later, I heard a rap on the front door.

"No, it isn't for the best," Zary said, storming into the living room. "You can't let this be it, Losha. You have to tell him."

"What if this was the universe telling me I shouldn't?"

"Do you really believe that nonsense?"

"Maybe."

"The timing is off. After everything has settled down with his father, you two can talk."

"We'll see."

15

Shiver

"Thornton, thank God you're home." My mother held her hand out to me. I bent down and kissed her cheek.

"How are you holding up, Duchess?"

"He asked for you, Thornton."

I took a step back. "He did? When?"

"About an hour ago," said Wilder, walking up behind me. "Go see him, Shiv."

I stopped briefly to hug my brother and then went in to see my father.

Before I left for the States, the duke hadn't been able to speak. When Wilder called, he said that our father had slipped into a coma. Things must have changed drastically for the better if he'd been able to speak well enough to ask for me.

When I opened the door to my father's bedchamber, I didn't know what I'd expected to see. Perhaps the duke sitting up and demanding someone read him the paper. Instead, he didn't look any different than he had before I left for the States.

I sat by my father's bedside and took his frail hand in mine.

The duke opened his eyes and turned his head. "Thornton," he whispered. "I'm so glad you've come."

"Of course, Father. I came as soon as Sutton called."

"There's…something…I need…to tell you." He wheezed more than spoke, struggling for every breath.

"Go ahead, Father. I'm here."

"I…love you…Thornton."

"I love you too, Father."

"I need…to tell you…"

"Tell me what?"

"Matthew…"

"Matthew?"

"I'm…sorry…wrong…find him…I need…stop him…before it's…too late."

"Father, who is Matthew?"

"He's…he's…"

The duke's eyes closed, and soon he was snoring softly, but I didn't leave. I'd sit here all night so I'd be here when my father woke again and could tell me who Matthew was and why I had to find him.

I leaned forward, rested my head on the bedside, and closed my eyes. I was exhausted—physically, mentally, and emotionally. The duke had been ill for so long that it was hard not to consider him passing away a blessing. But hearing him speak, hearing my father tell me he loved me, hearing his voice one more time—I'd do anything to bring the duke back to the way he was before the first stroke. If only I could.

I felt equally powerless to do anything about the situation with Losha. The entire flight home, I'd mulled over Gunner's words. Was Kazmir my child? If so, why in the name of God hadn't she told me? Why had she remained in hiding, particularly from me? That made the least sense. I could understand why she might've while United Russia's bounty was still active, but once it had been released, why hadn't she contacted me?

I'd asked myself the same questions again and again over the last twelve hours, and I still had no answers. Only Losha could give those to me, and it wasn't the kind of conversation we could have over the phone.

I had to be with her when I asked, looking into her eyes, and most importantly, making sure she didn't leave again. The thought of her disappearing, taking

Kazmir with her, tore at my heart. I wouldn't be able to bear it.

But now, I was needed here with my family. The duke needed me, and so did the duchess, Sutton, and Darrow. As hard as it would be, my conversation with Losha would have to wait.

I raised my head when I thought I felt my father's hand move.

Wilder stood next to me. "He's gone."

I looked up at my father's pale and lifeless body. "No, it can't be," I cried. "I've been right here."

I looked from my father to my brother. "How could I have slept? How could I not know he slipped away?"

"It's okay, Thornton," said my mother. "He was waiting for you so he could say goodbye."

My eyes filled with tears, and I rested my head back on the bedside. While I slept, my father died. What kind of man was I?

"Darrow?"

"She arrived not long after you. She came in, but didn't want to wake you."

"Why not? Oh, God, how could I have fallen asleep?" I cried again.

"Thornton, stop this. Your father saw you were here. Your presence gave him the peace he needed to let go of this life and move on to the next."

"Duchess," I said, standing to hug my mother. "I am so very sorry."

When I let her go, she bent over to kiss her husband's brow. "Godspeed, my love," she whispered.

My eyes met Wilder's. Our father was gone, and I'd been asleep when he passed away.

"Come now," my mother said, taking each of our hands and leading us from the room.

When we walked into the hallway, I saw my sister, tears streaming down her cheeks.

"Thornton," she cried, running into my arms.

"It's okay, sweet pea. He's in a better place now. One where he's no longer in pain, no longer suffering."

She pulled back and looked into my eyes. "He smiled at me. I know he did. When I went in to see him, he smiled."

"He loved you so much."

Wilder rested his hand on my arm. "There are calls to be made."

"Right," I said. "Darrow?"

"Go ahead." She wiped away her tears and put her arm through our mother's.

I watched them walk down the hallway and into the duchess' chambers.

"Wild, did the duke say anything to you about someone named Matthew?" I asked after making sure our mother and sister were far enough away that they wouldn't hear.

"Matthew? No. Why?"

"He was trying to tell me something, but then…"

"He only said two things to me, Shiv. The first was that he loved me, and the second was to ask for you."

"I'm so glad you were able to speak with him one last time, Wild."

"I wish Darrow had."

"Me too, but it sounds like his smile said everything he couldn't."

Wilder nodded. "We need to call the vicar. He was here earlier. And the undertaker."

"Would you like me to call both?"

Wilder shook his head. "I'll call the vicar."

As I was finishing the call to arrange for funeral services, my mother and Darrow came downstairs and went into the drawing room. Something told me I shouldn't ask my mother who Matthew was or why my father wanted me to find him.

"You're the duke now," she said when I joined them.

"Yes, Duchess."

"There are responsibilities that go along with the dukedom that I expect you're ready to take over."

"Mother, please," said Darrow. "Father has just passed."

The duchess' eyes grew heavy. Something more than the duke's passing troubled her. Could it be related to the mysterious Matthew?

"A word, Shiver, if you wouldn't mind," I heard Pinch say from the main entryway.

"I'm sorry to hear about the duke. My father asked me to send his condolences," Pinch said as I walked out of the drawing room.

"Of course, thank you, and please tell Wellie he's welcome to come up to the main house. You both are."

"I…uh…"

I followed Pinch's line of sight to where the duchess stood, scowling at us. I pulled Pinch around the corner.

"There's something we need to discuss, but this isn't the right time," I told him.

"Understood."

"I'll come by your father's place in an hour."

"I'll meet you there, and again, I'm sorry about the duke."

I put my hand on Pinch's shoulder. "I appreciate it."

"Hell of a way to start the new year," commented Wilder, joining us in the hallway.

"What's that?"

"It's New Year's Day. Hell of a thing."

I nodded. It was a hell of a thing.

"Am I interrupting?" Wilder asked.

"No. I was telling Pinch there's something we need to discuss. We'll meet at Wellie's cottage in an hour."

"I'm off, then." Pinch turned to leave.

"I'll walk you out," said Darrow, joining us in the entryway and touching Pinch's arm.

"What the bloody hell was that all about?" Wilder whispered.

I shrugged. I had far more to worry about than why Darrow wanted to walk Pinch to his car. I followed my brother back to our mother's drawing room, where I saw the duchess was still standing near the window.

"I want you to put a stop to that immediately," she spat.

"Duchess?"

"Darrow and the groundskeeper's son."

"Mother, you can't be serious," gasped Wilder. "The groundskeeper's son? She walked him out. I doubt that means they'll be announcing their engagement."

"You heard me," she said, glaring at both of us. "I want it stopped."

"Yes, Duchess," I answered, although I had no intention of following through on her demand.

When Wild turned and looked at me, I shook my head.

"Perhaps you'd like to rest. Sutton and I will let you be."

"Sutton, if you don't mind, I'd like a word with your brother."

"Certainly," he answered, looking all too pleased about having an excuse to leave.

"Sit, Thornton."

"Duchess, while I respect you very much, I must insist you remember that I am a human being, not a pet."

Rather than apologize as I'd anticipated she would, she folded her arms and stared at me until I took a seat.

"What is this really about, Mother?"

"A dalliance between your sister and that boy is something I can't abide."

Dalliance? Boy? I felt as though I'd entered an alternate universe. "Please elaborate, Mother."

She looked back out the window.

"You can't throw down a gauntlet such as that and walk away, Duchess. Tell me what's behind this."

"It's unseemly. Isn't that answer enough?"

"No, not even close. To begin, who says there's anything between them other than a lifelong friendship. And Axel, by the way, is a fine person as well as an esteemed member of SIS."

"What he does for a living, and even what kind of person you believe he is, has no bearing on this. It needs to stop, and that is my final word on the matter."

"I'll speak with her."

"I warn you, Thornton. If it does not, I'll be forced to tell Mr. Fulton to find another place of employment."

"Wellie?"

She scoffed at my use of the nickname, but nodded.

If my mother's behavior wasn't so extreme, I might've thought this was a manipulation designed to prod me into accepting my role as duke.

"I'll not allow it, Mother."

The duchess paled to the point I worried she might faint.

"Enough of this shroud of mystery, Mother. Explain this to me."

"There is nothing to explain," she muttered, leaving the room. "And Thorton." She stepped back inside the doorway. "It's time you resigned your position with MI6."

I grabbed my coat; I needed fresh air and to get away from the oppressive mood of the duchess. Her behavior was baffling. She'd gone from a woman deeply saddened by her husband's illness and subsequent death to a damn tyrant.

Her reaction to a possible relationship between Darrow and Pinch was so far out of character, it jarred me. That, coupled with my father's insistence that I look for someone named Matthew, was the reason I was out walking the estate that now, at least temporarily, was mine.

I'd every intention of reworking the terms of what would become my trust. I'd met with a solicitor five years ago when I couldn't bear the notion of leaving SIS.

Now, my desire to amend the estate's ownership had little to do with my work. More, it was the idea that there was a slim chance Gunner was right, and Kazmir was my child. If that was true, the life I would build with Losha might be very different than the one I'd lived as a child. Would she want to live on the English countryside in a home that was nothing like anything she'd ever known? It would be daunting for just about everyone, but especially her. She'd made her worry known that she'd never fit into my world, and while I didn't agree, I wouldn't force her to do anything she didn't want to do.

I closed my eyes, tamping down the dream of us spending our lives together, raising Kazmir. If it turned out my initial belief that Losha was involved with another man proved correct, the pain would be even more unbearable if I allowed myself to hope otherwise.

I approached the cottage where Wellie had lived since before I was born, and knocked on the door.

"Thornton," Wellie said, motioning for me to come in. "I am so sorry to hear of the duke's passing."

"Thank you, Wellie."

"Come in and tell me what brings you to my cottage."

I sat where Wellie pointed.

"Cup of tea?"

"Something a bit stronger if you have it."

The bottle Wellie set on the table in front of me was unmarked, but I could guess at its contents.

The old man sat and poured two glasses. "To our dear departed, that the devil mightn't hear of his death till he's safe inside the walls of heaven."

I downed the shot all at once, warmed by its potency. "Is this of your making?" I asked.

Wellie nodded. "'Twas your father's favorite."

"I want to talk to you about the last thing my father said to me before he died."

Wellie raised a brow.

"He mentioned the name Matthew and told me to find him."

Wellie's eyes hooded. "What else did he say?"

"To find him before it's too late. Do you know who Matthew is, Wellie?"

The man shook his head. "I cannot say."

I poured another shot and downed it. "You forget what I do for a living, my friend. You cannot say or you won't say, is entirely different than not knowing."

"It isn't my story to tell, Thornton," he said before walking out the door of the cottage.

Within a number of minutes, the door reopened; Pinch and Wilder came inside.

"Where's my father?"

"He left."

Pinch raised a brow like his father had.

"I told him that my father mentioned someone named Matthew and asked me to find him. Any idea who that is?"

Pinch shook his head.

"Your father knows something that he isn't willing to talk about."

"What did he say?"

"That it wasn't his story to tell."

This time Pinch nodded.

I looked at Wilder, whose eyes told me that he too believed both Pinch and Wellie knew more than they were willing to say.

Before I left, I picked up the unmarked bottle of booze and took it back to the abbey with me.

16

Losha

"Happy New Year," said Zary, coming in the front door. "I hope you don't mind me doing that. I guess I shouldn't just use your code to walk into your house."

I smiled. "Happy New Year to you as well. As far as you walking in, if there is a time that I'm concerned with my privacy, I'll let you know."

"You could always just throw the latch," said Gunner, coming in behind Zary. "She won't get past that."

I looked to where Gunner was pointing, and saw that there were two latches at the top and bottom of the door, which would keep an intruder out even if they did have the code to the keypad. I doubted I'd ever have a need to use either, but was glad he'd shown them to me.

"Thanks," I murmured. "But Zary, as she so often reminds me, is my closest friend, and I'll remind you both, this is not my house."

"It is while you're staying here," responded Gunner.

I smiled again. "You really are too kind to me."

Zary put her arms around Gunner's waist.

"What would you like to do today?" he asked.

"I was thinking Kazmir might like to see the elephant seals," said Zary.

"Elephant seals?"

"There's a rookery a few miles north of here, near the Piedras Blancas lighthouse."

Kazmir giggled and pointed and tried to squirm out of my arms as we stood near the fence that overlooked the beach where more than one hundred elephant seals bathed in the sunlight.

I laughed. "They're so loud."

"Is the baby warm enough?" Gunner asked.

His cheeks were pink, but I doubted Kazmir was cold. "It's far colder in Lapland," I told him.

"Is that where you were?"

"Part of the time."

I looked past Gunner and saw a dark-colored car entering the parking lot. Something about it raised my hackles. "I'm getting a little chilly, though," I said, not wanting to elevate undue suspicion, but also anxious to leave as soon as possible.

We weren't parked too far away, but even with the short walk, it would've been enough time for whomever was in the car to get out. And they hadn't.

"Everything okay?" Zary asked as I buckled Kazmir into the car seat.

I nodded and glanced over at the car. Zary followed my line of sight and nodded as well.

I put Kazmir down for a nap, hoping he woke early enough that he wouldn't fight going to sleep later tonight, and went out to the kitchen, but wasn't hungry enough to bother making anything. I heard my phone's vibrations and looked around but couldn't remember where I'd put it. I finally found it on the dresser in the bedroom, but not quickly enough. I checked the log and saw I'd missed a call from Shiver.

Before I could talk myself out of it, I rang him back.

"Losha," he said, answering before the phone finished its first ring. "I so needed to hear your voice."

Shiver sounded drunk, a state I hadn't seen him in very often, but under the circumstances, he was certainly entitled to be.

"How are you?" I asked. "How is your father?"

"He died, Losha. Last night, while I slept, he died."

"I'm sorry, Shiver."

"I fell asleep and he died."

I wasn't sure what to say or why Shiver was so upset that his father had passed while he slept.

"I'm such a bloody bastard."

"Shiver, I'm sure you were very tired."

"I rested my head on his bedside and fell asleep. He might as well have been alone for all the good my being there did."

I took a deep breath; I was beginning to understand. "He knew you were with him. I'm sure it brought him great comfort."

"I need you, Losha. Why wouldn't you come with me?"

"You didn't ask."

"Would you have?"

God, I hated to upset him further when he was drunk, but I couldn't pile on another lie. "No, I wouldn't have."

"I love you, Losha. I love you so much, and I know that I've just met him for the first time, but I love Kazmir too. Let me take care of you. Whether he's my child or not. Let me love you both. Do you love me, Losha? Even a little?"

I gasped and closed my eyes. Would he even remember this conversation? Would he remember saying he loved Kazmir—his son? Was this the right time to tell him the baby was his? If he were in front of me, I'd throw my arms around him and tell him I loved him too. How could I not when he'd just asked me to let him love us both? But what if he didn't remember this conversation tomorrow? I couldn't risk it. Instead, I repeated the words I'd said to him before.

"With all my heart, Shiver," I whispered, not sure I wanted him to hear, but powerless not to answer when he sounded in such pain.

"That's what you said about Kazmir's father. How can you love two men with all your heart?"

"I can't."

"Oh, God," he cried. "I didn't want to do this over the phone, but is he mine, Losha?"

My eyes filled with tears as I cursed myself for calling him back. This couldn't be the way I told him Kazmir was his. "I have to go, Shiver. If you remember this conversation, call me back tomorrow."

When I disconnected the call, I blocked his number. Tomorrow, once Shiver had a chance to sober up, I'd unblock it.

17

Shiver

I rolled over and shrouded my eyes from the light coming in the bedroom window.

What in God's name had I done last night? I peered at the night table with one eye and saw the empty bottle of Wellie's brandy. Jesus, I'd drunk the whole thing.

My mouth felt as though it was filled with cotton balls, my head throbbed, and my body felt too heavy to even sit up. I closed one eye, opened the other, and looked down at what I was wearing. For the second time in as many weeks, I'd fallen asleep without removing my shoes. What the hell was wrong with me?

I groaned when the throbbing in my head intensified, and thought of Losha, like I always did. Whether it brought me intense pain or immeasurable pleasure, I couldn't stop her image from appearing at the forefront of my mind. The image of her had changed, though. Now, instead of just Losha, the picture that first came to me was of her, sitting in front of me, the baby nursing at her breast. I still could not imagine a more beautiful sight.

When I reached for the phone to check the time, my finger brushed the call log button by mistake.

"What's this?" I muttered to myself. There was an unanswered call from me to Losha at one in the morning, followed by a call back from her that had lasted almost ten minutes.

I had no recollection of it whatsoever. What the hell had I said to her?

The days that followed my drunken night were filled with people coming and going for the duke's visitation, wake, and burial on the grounds of Whittaker Abbey. I woke as exhausted as I went to bed each night. My mother's mood hadn't changed, but like all well-bred English women, she hid it well in the face of visitors.

Pinch appeared to be keeping his distance from Darrow. I had no idea if that was out of a sense of propriety or if the duchess had said something to one or both of them.

And Wellie? He kept his distance from her as well.

My phone vibrated in my pocket, and I stepped out of the room where the duchess was conversing with visitors, and into the main hall.

"Hello, sir," I answered when I saw it was Rivet calling.

"Shiv, I was so sorry to hear of the duke's passing. I'm on holiday and have been out of touch, but that's no excuse."

"Please don't apologize. I appreciate your call, Riv."

"That isn't my only reason for getting in touch with you. When I called Patsy to check in, she told me about your father. She also told me that there was a high alert issued for K19's Dutch Miller."

Dutch Miller? How long was it since I'd last seen him with Mantis and Alegria? A handful of days? What the hell had happened? "I'm sorry, I didn't know either."

"I figured as much. However, I'd like you to pass something on to Doc Butler if you would."

"Of course."

"I'm in Kaiserslautern, Germany, on holiday as I said, and I strongly believe I spotted him last evening."

"You saw Dutch in Germany?"

"Again, I was unaware of the alert at the time, and now I feel as though I've been derelict in my report."

"You couldn't know what you didn't know, Riv."

"As it was, I suppose you're right, but please do pass the word on to Doc or whomever you happen to speak with."

"Have you contacted him?"

"I have but haven't yet heard back."

"I'll see if I can reach him."

"Much appreciated, Shiver. Again, I'm sorry to hear of your father's passing. I regret that I won't be there for the services."

I ended the call and immediately called Doc to pass word on about Dutch. Doc offered condolences from Merrigan and himself.

"What's going on?" I asked, thinking better of it after it was too late.

"Dutch went undercover, but we lost track of him. Now that we have some idea of his twenty, we'll send a team in."

I didn't ask anything more. I knew enough just by Doc's tone to suggest that whatever Dutch was in the middle of, it was imperative Doc act on it immediately.

18

Losha

On the seventh day after Shiver's call, it dawned on me that I'd never unblocked his number. Initially, I'd only wanted to avoid him calling back while still drunk. I'd fully intended to unblock the number the next day, but completely forgot.

Even if he had called, now I'd never know it unless he'd left a message. Disappointed when there wasn't one, I wondered if I should call him. How much of our conversation did he even remember, given how drunk he was?

I startled when I heard a knock at the door. When I opened it, instead of Zary, Gunner stood on the other side.

"Is everything okay?"

"I'm leaving in a little over an hour."

"I see. Is there anything I can do?"

"I'd like Zary to stay over here while I'm gone. I'd say you should stay in our side of the duplex, but it would be harder to move all of Kazmir's things. Would you mind?"

"Not at all."

"Thanks, Orina. I'll be back as soon as I can."

"I know better than to ask, but is it bad?"

"A couple members of our crew have gotten themselves in pretty deep water. I wouldn't go otherwise."

I nodded, understanding everything he didn't say. It wasn't just deep water; they had to be drowning.

"I wanted to ask you first before I talked to Zary about staying here."

"Tell her it's to keep me company."

Gunner smiled. "Thanks. That was my plan."

For a moment, I wondered if I should tell Gunner about my unease earlier in the week when we went to see the elephant seals, but decided against it. Zary had likely already mentioned it, and if members of their team were in trouble, he didn't need another worry on his shoulders.

Within a half hour, Zary walked through the front door, looking as though she'd been crying.

"What's happened?" I gasped.

She waved her hand in front of her face. "I almost don't recognize myself sometimes. I get so emotional. Ava said it's the pregnancy hormones."

I remembered being emotional when I was pregnant too, but I hadn't attributed it to hormones. Instead, I'd been running for my life and that of my son at the time, with absolutely no one to turn to, certainly not my baby's father or a half sister.

"I'm sorry," Zary apologized. "I didn't mean to make you angry. I do that a lot."

"You didn't, and you don't," I lied, trying to shrug off the feeling of envy that crept in so often. "Come here and sit with me." I motioned toward the sofa.

Zary sat and folded her arms.

"I'm not angry with you; it's just that there are times that I feel very alone in the world."

"You have me."

"I do. And you have Gunner, your mother, your sisters…"

"I can't apologize for that, Losha."

"I'm not suggesting you should. In fact, if there is anyone I'm angry with, it's myself. I don't begrudge you any happiness, Zary. I'm just feeling sorry for myself."

"Have you heard from Shiver?"

I shook my head. I hadn't told Zary about his drunken phone call and didn't plan to now. "Something's just occurred to me," I said instead. "Where's your mother now?"

"She's with Madeline, Gunner's mother. They're planning the wedding."

"Your wedding?"

Zary nodded. "Thankfully, yes. I'm completely overwhelmed with my life as it is."

"What do you mean?"

"Just because I seem happy doesn't mean that I don't have anxiety, Losha. It isn't easy to go from having no one, as you said, to finding out my mother, who I believed died when I was a child, is still alive, or that I have half sisters. Gunner has been great about letting me take things at a pace I'm comfortable with. In fact, that's one of the reasons he suggested we come here."

"I'm sorry, I didn't think—"

"The truth is, the reason I'm truly happy is because you're here. And Gunner, of course. With you, I don't have to pretend that I have the slightest clue about being a mother or a daughter or even a sister. I can relax and just be myself, and no one is going to judge me for not knowing how to make scrambled eggs."

"Wow."

Zary huffed. "What?"

"Now I really feel like a *mudak*."

Zary laughed. "You should feel *better*."

Strangely, I did. Knowing Zary hadn't just woken up to a perfect life, made me feel less sorry for myself, although not so much less of a *zhopa* about it.

"Do you think Kazmir would be up for a walk in town later?"

"I'm sure he'd be up for a ride in the pram. Oh, I've been meaning to ask—did you mention what happened the other day to Gunner?"

Zary's eyes darkened. "No. I decided to wait to see if it occurred again. Do you think I should have?"

"No. It was probably nothing. I've been on the run so long, it's hard to let go of the paranoia."

"The paranoia kept us alive, Losha."

"I'm starving," I told Zary later after we'd walked from one end of the town to the other. "Should we go back to the house?"

"What, and cook?"

We both laughed.

"There are so many places to eat in Cambria. I think we should go to a different restaurant every night while Gunner is gone."

"Sounds good to me."

"Let's start at the north end and work our way to the south. If we eat out for lunch too, we can probably get through them all."

"And put on twenty pounds." I'd been itching to start training again. I'd begun feeding Kazmir baby food, which meant he could go longer between nursing. "You don't need to worry about it, but I do. I think it's part of my problem; I don't feel great about myself."

"You have a full workout room downstairs."

"I do?"

Zary nodded.

"Downstairs?"

"Yes, haven't you been in the basement?"

"No. I didn't know there was a basement."

"I'll show you later."

"It's this way," said Zary after we got back, and she opened a door that I hadn't noticed before.

"What is that?" she asked when we heard beeping.

"I have no idea."

"Is it part of an alarm system?"

"I don't know why there would be one separate of the main house."

I walked in the direction of the beeping and froze. *"Get out!"* I screamed. *"Get Kazmir!"*

"What is it?"

"A bomb!"

19

Shiver

"Thornton, may I speak with you?"

"Of course, Duchess." I followed her into the duke's study.

"It is time for you to take over the management of the estate." She pointed to a row of cabinets and opened the first. "You'll find the annual reports in here."

One by one, she opened doors, explaining what was to be found behind each one. "There's much for you to get caught up on."

"Duchess, I spoke with Darrow and Sutton before Father passed. The three of us will be hiring an estate manager soon."

"What?" she gasped.

"Even Father didn't do it all on his own, and you know it." I took her hand, led her out of the study and into one of the formal drawing rooms, and closed the door behind us.

"I'm worried about you, Mother. While it's some-what to be expected, you aren't acting yourself."

"You should be focused on your responsibilities, not on me."

"See? That's exactly what I'm talking about. I am over thirty years old, and I don't remember a single time in my life when you spoke to me in that tone of voice."

"You have a poor memory."

"I do not. And you are a lousy liar. So let's get straight to it. What's wrong?"

She stood and walked over to the window. "Just because your father is dead, doesn't give you the right to upend my life."

"No one is upending your life. On the contrary. Sutton, Darrow, and I intend to do everything in our power to keep your life exactly as it's always been."

"Keeping my life as it's been is *not* in your power. If that were the case, I wouldn't be a widow."

"Duchess—"

"No, Thornton. Whatever you have to say, I refuse to listen. Your father worked hard his entire life, as did his father before him, and so on. I will not allow you to throw away your birthright. Nor will I allow Darrow to throw away her chance of marrying well.

Who will want her once they find out she's been with the groundskeeper's son?"

"You can't be serious."

"I am. Very serious."

My phone vibrated, but I ignored it. Within seconds, it vibrated again.

"Should you answer?"

"No. It can wait until we finish this conversation."

When my phone went off a third time, I pulled it out of my pocket, stunned to see that the calls I'd missed in such close succession were from Zary. "Forgive me, but I fear there's an emergency."

She nodded, and I stepped out of the room.

Zary picked up, but I couldn't make out a word she was saying.

"Slow down, I can't understand you," I shouted into the phone. The only word I heard loud and clear made my blood turn to ice. *"Bomb!"*

Zary calmed down enough to tell me that they'd discovered a bomb in the basement and that she, Losha, and Kazmir had immediately left. She also told me Gunner was in Afghanistan with almost all of the K19 team.

"I don't know where to go," she cried.

"Try to stay calm. Where are you now?"

"Driving through the village."

"There's a safe house in Harmony. It's about fifteen minutes south of Cambria. Set your GPS, and I'll call you back with the access code in less than ten minutes. It'll take you longer than that to get there. Is anyone following you?"

"I don't think so."

"You know what to do, Zary. Both you and Losha do. Focus, and get to the safe house. Help will be on its way."

The first person I contacted when I ended the call with Zary was Wilder. "I need you here, now! Where are you?"

"I'm at Wellie's. What's wrong, Shiv?"

"I'll explain when you get here. Bring Pinch."

Next, I called Rivet, who would have easier access to someone at the CIA.

Doc was gone, but Merrigan wasn't. I called her and explained I'd told Zary to head to the Harmony safe house.

"That's the best place for them for now," she said. "If you can arrange transport that will guarantee their safety, tomorrow they should head here. I'll call Zary directly as soon as I've reprogrammed the access code."

"Mer? We also need to call a bomb squad."

"On it."

I hung up and called Zary back. "Hang tight. Merrigan will call you in a matter of minutes. Still no one following you?"

"Not that Losha or I have been able to pick up on."

"May I speak with her?"

"Of course."

"Hi," she said, her voice shaky.

"How are you holding up?"

"Terrified. Furious."

"Both to be expected."

"Shiv, there's another call coming in."

"I'm on my way. I'll get there as soon as I can." I heard the familiar sound of the call ending.

"Thornton?"

I closed my eyes, realizing my mother had overheard me. "I don't have time to explain right now, but I will, Duchess. I promise."

Wilder and Pinch rushed through the door. "What's happening?" my brother asked.

"Come with me," I told them. As hard as it was to do, I had to leave my mother standing in the main hall.

I closed the door to the duke's study and briefed them about what I knew so far.

"United Russia?" Pinch asked.

"My first thought, but there's no way to know for sure at this point."

"The entire K19 team is in Afghanistan?" Wilder asked.

"Everyone but Merrigan and Mercer Bryant, who is in Turks and Caicos on holiday with his wife and out of contact. Rivet is reaching out to the agency to see who they can send and how quickly."

"What about you?"

"I'm leaving as soon as I can make arrangements."

"Where do you want me?" asked Pinch.

"With me. Wild, you stay here. Riv will clear you to be away from MI5 until further notice."

"Understood."

"I need to talk to the duchess before I go."

Wilder nodded.

"I'll grab my gear and meet you back here," said Pinch, leaving the room.

"Thornton, what's going on?" my mother asked when I came back into the drawing room and found her pacing in front of the fireplace.

"I don't have a lot of time to explain."

She nodded.

"There's a situation in the States that requires SIS support. I need to leave immediately."

"What about your responsibilities here?"

I took a deep breath. "I simply cannot get into this with you now."

"Where are you going?"

"I've already answered that question." I kissed both her cheeks. "I'll be in touch."

"Godspeed, Thornton."

"Thank you, Duchess."

20

Losha

"Hello, Merrigan? It's Losha," I said after ending my call with Shiver to answer this one.

"I have your code. Are you ready?"

"Go ahead."

Merrigan rattled off a series of numbers and letters.

"Got it. Thank you."

"As I told Shiver, you're to stay in the Harmony safe house tonight, but in the morning, I want you to come here to Montecito. In the meantime, I'm doing everything I can to reach Doc or Gunner."

"I…um…my baby."

"Yes, I know, Losha. We are fully equipped here for your little boy. Call me after you've arrived at the safe house."

"Still no sign we're being followed," Zary reported. "We're almost there."

We'd had to flee the house without grabbing anything other than our wallets and Kazmir's diaper bag, and only because they were sitting near the door.

Everything else we needed, we'd have to figure out a way to secure.

As soon as we were off the highway, Zary cut the lights on the car and followed the directions on the GPS to the house.

I called in the code to the number Merrigan had given me, and within seconds, the garage door opened and a gate I hadn't seen, closed behind us. By the time the car was fully inside the garage, that door had closed as well.

"Have you heard of Burns Butler?" Zary asked as I punched the code into the keypad by the door that led into the house.

"Sounds familiar."

"He's Doc's father."

This was a little bit too much for me to process at the moment, but I remembered Shiver mentioning something about the infamous CIA agent, who was a legend in the intelligence community, having a connection to Doc and K19 Security Solutions.

"He's the one who set up this safe house."

Given Zary sounded as though that was significant, I guessed that meant we didn't need to worry about our safety tonight.

When her phone buzzed, Zary answered it.

"Yes. We're here, Merrigan. I was just about—"

I couldn't hear what Merrigan was saying but watched Zary's expression change from concerned to calm. Something had happened; maybe Merrigan was able to reach Gunner.

"Speak of the devil," Zary said when she hung up.

"What does that mean?"

"Burns is on his way here now. Change of plans. We aren't going to Montecito."

"Where are we going?"

"Butler Ranch."

"What is that?"

"Burns' family has a vineyard and winery not far from here. I've heard it's quite breathtaking."

I sat in a chair by the table and looked through Kazmir's diaper bag. "I only have two diapers with me, and no baby food for him."

"I'm sorry, Losha."

"Don't be. It isn't your fault. I think we can make it through the night, but tomorrow I'll have to get to a store."

"Perhaps Burns can help."

"How?"

"He probably knows where to buy diapers."

"Right."

"Oh, Merrigan also said that there was a bomb squad at the house."

I closed my eyes, shuddered, and said a prayer of thanks that Zary had decided to show me the workout room. If she hadn't, all three of us would likely be dead by now.

Zary sat in one of the other chairs. "Are you okay?"

"I should never have come out of hiding."

"I'm sorry, Losha," Zary said a second time.

"Again, it isn't your fault. You believed the bounty was lifted. It might be for you, but I fear it's a different story for me."

"You can't know that for sure."

I stood with Kazmir in my arms. "It isn't just me, Zary. I have to protect my son."

"What are you going to do?"

"I don't know yet. Right now, I'm going to nurse Kazmir in the other room." I walked out of the kitchen and into what looked like a living room. I had nowhere for the baby to sleep tonight, two diapers, no food, and I'd almost gotten my son killed. I was a terrible mother. On top of everything else, I was selfish because even if it would ensure his safety, there was no way I could give him up.

I overheard Zary talking to a man who I assumed was Burns, but since Kazmir was still nursing, I stayed where I was while straining to hear what the two were discussing.

"We'll leave as soon as Losha is ready," I heard the man say.

Tonight? I'd somehow gotten the impression we wouldn't leave until tomorrow, but did it really matter? Regardless of when we left or where we went, I would be at the mercy of someone other than myself for our protection—not something I was accustomed to.

The other thing I overheard the man say was that the bomb had been diffused. It was a relief that not only had the duplex been spared, but if they were able to inspect the device, it might give clues as to who'd planted it.

When Kazmir fell asleep, I refastened the maternity bra, closed my blouse, and carried the baby into the kitchen.

"Losha. May I call you that?" the man asked, holding out his hand.

"Of course."

"I'm Laird Butler, known to some as Burns."

"It's an honor to meet you, sir."

"The honor is mine," he responded. "Who is this?" he said, peering at the baby in my arms.

"This is Kazmir, who has a very full tummy at the moment."

"He's beautiful," said Burns. "Shall we be on our way? Sorcha is busy setting up a nursery. Our daughter brought some of their baby-related items to the ranch."

I felt my cheeks pinken. "We don't want to be a bother."

"Not at all. She isn't using them presently. Is there anything else you can think of you'll need straight off?"

"As I told Zary, Kazmir will need diapers."

"Done, or it will be as soon as I know what type you prefer." Burns laughed. "Don't look so surprised, lass. Sorcha and I are grandparents above all else at this time in our lives."

"Thank you so much," I murmured, having a hard time marrying the kindly "grandfather" standing in front of me with the infamous Burns Butler.

It took a half hour to drive from the safe house to the ranch via the back roads of the wine country. Since we didn't see a single other car the entire way, I gathered Burns took the route intentionally. It would've been evident if someone were following us.

"Here we are," he said, waiting for the ranch gate to open. "We'll go to the main house first so Sorcha can make sure you have everything you need that she's certain I've forgotten. Our son Naughton and his wife live in it now, and we live in one of the smaller cottages, but the main house still serves as a gathering place."

While I couldn't see much in the dark, the moonlight illuminated the rows and rows of grapevines as we drove the dirt road leading to several structures that looked like homes straight out of Scotland.

"My father bought the land with the money he made working for Randolph Hearst when he constructed what most call Hearst Castle, but he referred to as *'La Cuesta Encantada.'*"

"The Enchanted Hill," I muttered.

"You know it, then."

"Just the translation."

"I've heard you're a linguist."

Burns had heard of me? "Languages come easy to me."

Zary's phone vibrated, startling me. "There's a message from Merrigan saying she's reached Doc. She said I should expect to hear from Gunner later tonight or in the morning. Have you heard anything more from Shiver?" Zary whispered.

I shook my head. All he'd said before I had to quickly end the call was that he was on his way.

I had no idea what to expect once he arrived. I'd surmised he remembered nothing of the conversation we'd had when he was drunk.

Given the plan I'd begun formulating involved informing Shiver that Kazmir and I would be connecting with the baby's father, who had offered us his protection, the less he remembered from that night's conversation, the better.

I hadn't determined yet where I'd go or what I'd do once I got there since my plan was merely an elaborate lie. My money wouldn't last much more than a year, and that was only if I was very frugal with it.

Other than having a knack for assassinating United Russia's enemies, my job skills were sorely lacking. Not that I'd be able to find employment that would allow me to have Kazmir with me, and there would be no way I'd let anyone else care for my child. The risk that he would be abducted, or worse, was far too great.

"Come in, come in," said the woman with the heavy Scottish accent that I guessed was Sorcha Butler, herding us in the front door.

Once inside the main room of the house, I saw two boxes of diapers along with baby clothes, blankets, and several types of baby food.

"There's more in the cottage where you'll be staying, lass," Sorcha explained. "However, I'm sure the bairn will need some of this now."

"Sorcha, you'll overwhelm the lass." I heard Burns scold his wife.

"Actually, he does need a diaper change. Is there a place I can do it?"

Sorcha plucked a diaper out, grabbed a box of baby wipes, a blanket, and a sleeper gown. "This way," she said, leading me through the house. "That's my dear daughter-in-law Bradley," Sorcha said, motioning to the woman standing near the stove in the kitchen. "Bradley, this is Losha. I'll let you two chat once she's changed the baby."

The woman smiled and waved. "Nice to meet you, Losha."

My chest felt tight, not because they weren't all very nice, but this was the kind of family I thought only existed in the books I'd read while Kazmir and I hid out in one European country after another. Reading made me both yearn for a family for Kazmir and not believe they existed.

"Bradley and Naughton's wee one is just four months old, a boy they named Charlie."

While I changed Kazmir's diaper, Sorcha told me about the rest of her grandchildren, not that I'd remember, but it was pleasant to hear the woman speak so lovingly of her family.

"How old is Kazmir?" Sorcha asked.

"Just six months."

"Same age as my granddaughter, Coco. She's my son Maddox and his wife Alex's bairn." Sorcha cooed at the baby. "He's beautiful."

"Thank you." I picked him up and nuzzled his sweet neck. "He's a very happy baby."

When my eyes met Sorcha's, I recognized the longing. "Would you like to hold him?"

"Would make my heart so happy if you'd let me."

I smiled and handed Kazmir to her. Rather than reaching back for me or crying because he was in the arms of a stranger, my baby cooed and smiled.

"Grandma Sorcha will give your mum a wee break so we can have a chat," the woman babbled to Kazmir as they walked away.

"You'll never get him back," teased Bradley when I walked past the kitchen. "Although there's no better grandmum in the world."

"I believe it, even after a few minutes. Sorcha said you have a little boy too?"

Bradley smiled. "Charlie. Love of my life. He's out with his father now, who is the other love of my life."

Surrounded by a warm and welcoming family should calm me, if not make me happy. But it was the opposite, only serving to remind me that I had neither in my life, outside of Zary, whom I couldn't continue to take advantage of. She and Gunner had been so generous, but if the bomb was nothing else, it was a terrifying reminder that we, and everyone around us, were in danger. I couldn't expose Zary to it any longer. I had to leave as soon as I could make arrangements and it was safe to do so.

After a dinner during which I ate far too much, Burns led Kazmir, Zary, and me across a courtyard to a lovely cottage where he said one of his sons had lived before he got married.

It was sparsely furnished, like I imagined most men's homes would be, but had warmth too.

"What is it with these guys and their bathrooms?" said Zary as she walked down the staircase to where I sat nursing Kazmir one last time before I put him down for the night.

"The one upstairs has the most amazing shower I've ever seen."

"Yeah?"

"Seriously, Losha. Wait until you see it. By the way, there are two cribs already set up. One is in the master bedroom and the other is in the room across from it. I took the room down the hall."

"You can take the bigger room, I don't mind."

Zary rolled her eyes. "Don't be silly. What do I care?"

I checked the time, wondering if Shiver would arrive sometime tomorrow or if he was still in England. Not knowing meant I had to act at the first opportunity.

Once he got here, it would be harder to leave, both physically and emotionally.

"Zary, when you and Gunner were first together… was it difficult to accept his help when you wanted to leave UR?"

She laughed. "Actually, I begged him to help me. Although I know what you're asking. It was harder for me to trust that he would do it my way, if that makes sense."

I nodded. Both of us had been forced to be independent from a very young age—out of necessity.

"The harder part was trusting him with my mother."

"What do you mean?"

"I knew Gunner would help me, protect me, at all costs, but I didn't know if he'd do the same for my mother. That's what I struggled with. Trusting him with another person."

My fear exactly. I worried that Shiver wouldn't understand that if anything happened to Kazmir, I would no longer have a reason to live. Would he protect my baby with his life in the same way I would? Would he make decisions about our safety without my consent? That, I wouldn't be able to abide, regardless of how much he vowed to protect us.

It took me a minute to remember where I was when I opened my eyes to the sun streaming in through the window. Like the first morning I woke up in the house in Cambria, I was stunned by how well I'd slept. Kazmir was still sleeping soundly too.

I heard voices downstairs, but allowed myself to linger a little while longer in the warm cocoon of the most comfortable bed I'd ever slept in.

When I'd gone into the bathroom last night, I was astounded by what Zary had referred to as the most amazing shower she'd ever seen. Not only was the shower amazing, but there was what one might loosely refer to as a bathtub too.

The two-person jetted tub sat on the opposite side of the freestanding wall of a shower big enough that two or three people could stand in it. There was no shower head, but it looked as though water flowed from hundreds of pin-size openings in the ceiling. Should I take advantage of it, or the luxurious bath this morning?

I padded into the room, peeking at my sleeping baby on my way. Since I hadn't had time to grab the baby monitor, or much else, when we fled the house in fear for our lives, I kept the door open, hoping I'd hear him if he woke up and cried.

Looking around for a way to turn the water on, I found what appeared to be a control panel. I pushed the on/off button, and it lit up. There was an icon to choose the bath or shower along with a water-temperature control. As I experimented with the other options, the patterns and pressure of the water flowing from the ceiling changed, as did the jets of the tub.

I couldn't figure out what the second button called "heat" might be for, until I felt the tile warm beneath my feet.

If I were ever in the position of building a house and had an unlimited amount of money, I'd install a bathroom exactly like this one.

When I heard Kazmir fussing, I turned the water off and returned to the bedroom.

"Good morning, sweet baby boy," I said, lifting him out of the crib and kissing his cheek. "I bet you'd rather eat before your bath." I sat on the bed to let Kazmir nurse.

"Knock, knock," said Zary from outside the bedroom door.

"Come in."

"I heard the water going on and off, on and off," Zary teased.

"I was just about to take advantage of it when this one woke up."

"I can take him if you want. Sorcha is downstairs, making breakfast."

"She is?"

"I think she was hoping to spend time with the baby more than you or me."

I laughed. "She's very sweet."

Zary raised a brow.

"What?"

"I've heard stories to the contrary."

"Really? I'm intrigued."

"I bet if we asked, we could get her to tell us about her days as an intelligence operative."

As I shifted Kazmir off my breast, he fussed a little but stopped before it turned into a full-blown tantrum. When we got downstairs and he saw Sorcha's out-stretched arms, he smiled.

"Come see your grandmum, wee baby boy," she said, taking him from my arms.

Zary and I looked at each other and smiled.

"Bradley said you were the best grandmum in the world."

"Aye, lass, I am. Isn't that right?" she answered without taking her eyes off the baby.

"We were hoping you'd tell us a story of your days in the intelligence business," said Zary.

"Oh, goodness. I'm not sure the bairn would enjoy stories like that."

"Tell us how you met Burns. He'll like that story."

"I knew the minute I laid eyes on him that he was the one for me. I was in Ramstein hospital. 'Twas Burns that saved my life, although I *dinnae ken* until several days after the fact."

Sorcha sat at the table and bounced Kazmir on her lap. "I'd infiltrated the Provisional Irish Republican Army—most know it as the IRA. I was there on Bloody Friday, at the Oxford Street bus station." Sorcha showed us the scarring on her left arm. "I survived with these, and more on my back, but worse, we lost two agents in the blast."

I knew the story of the infamous day. A total of twenty-four bombs were planted in and around the city of Belfast by the IRA, killing nine and injuring well over a hundred. At least seventy of those severely injured were civilian women and children.

"In a little over an hour, those bastards turned Belfast into a war zone," Sorcha told us. "The bombs had been detonating that long when SIS got the intel that a warning had been sent to the Royal Ulster Constabulary about another bomb scheduled to detonate at Oxford Street, the busiest bus station in all of Northern Ireland." Sorcha shook her head. "The two we lost refused to evacuate and were searching for the bomb when it went off." She stood and walked over to the window. "But you asked me about Burns, didn't you?"

Zary and I both nodded.

"He was part of the team the agency sent in via heli. 'Twas him that carried me away from the blast."

"How did you end up in Ramstein?"

"He insisted I be transported there. I almost died several times due to infection, lass. If I had stayed in Belfast, it would've killed me if the IRA didn't first."

"Your cover was blown."

"Aye," said Sorcha, nodding. "He saved my life in more ways than one." She patted my hand. "That's enough about that."

"Gunner saved my life more than once," said Zary with tears in her eyes. "Sorry."

"Why on earth are you sorry, lass?" Sorcha asked.

"Pregnancy hormones," Zary answered, fanning her face. "I've never cried so much in my life."

Sorcha reached over and patted her hand too. "'Tis how women like us know."

"What do you mean?"

The woman nodded at Zary and then smiled at me. "There was only one man I trusted to protect me more than I could've on my own."

That may be true for Zary and Gunner and Sorcha and Burns, but that didn't make it true for Shiver and me.

"Let him in, lass. Let him take care of you," Sorcha said, making me wonder how the woman knew my thoughts.

"That's what I've told her," added Zary.

"You should listen to us," said Sorcha, standing to finish making breakfast with Kazmir in her arms.

"I'm so full," said Zary, rubbing her tummy after we'd finished breakfast and Sorcha left.

"Me too. What would you think about a walk in the vineyard?"

"I'd love it."

I went upstairs to grab the jacket that Bradley had lent me before we left the main house last night and to put Kazmir in one of the adorable outfits Sorcha and Burns' daughter had brought for him.

When I pulled a dark-green jacket out of the pile of clothes, Kazmir squealed.

"You like this?"

The baby waved his arms and squealed some more. He was such a happy baby, but more so since we'd arrived here the night before. Probably, like me, he was basking in the glow of love the family gave so easily. Would my love be enough for him after this? I shook my head. What choice did I have? It wasn't as though I could create an instant family for him. We would have to be enough for each other.

"Ready?" asked Zary from the hallway.

I wiped away my tears and plucked Kazmir out of the crib where I'd put him while I changed into some of the other clothes that had miraculously shown up here for me.

"Isn't it amazing?" Zary asked when we reached the top of a crest in the vineyards. From there we had a three-hundred-and-sixty-degree view of Butler Ranch as well as the surrounding ranches, all the way west to the Pacific Ocean.

"It isn't always this clear," said Burns, walking up from the other direction. "You picked a good day." He turned and took in the whole view like we had. "'Twas a perfect place for Sorcha and me to raise our family."

"How many children do you have?" I asked.

"Four boys and two girls," he beamed, counting on his fingers. "And five grandchildren, plus two more on the way."

"You and Sorcha are blessed."

"We are. As are you." Burns held his finger out, and Kazmir grasped it. "You hold the meaning of life in your arms. Whenever you find yourself forgetting, look into your wee one's eyes, and you'll remember."

"Thank you, Burns, for bringing us here. I can't tell you how much I appreciate it."

"You are welcome here anytime, my dear. I'm heading back to the house now. Walk with me?"

21

Shiver

"Pinch, we need to talk about Darrow, but please let me finish what I have to say before commenting."

The man, who felt more like my brother than the son of a hired hand at the estate or an MI6 subordinate, nodded.

"The duchess is having a problem with the idea of a relationship between the two of you. She made mention that if it continued, she'd have to let your father go."

Pinch nodded a second time.

"You don't seem surprised."

"She told me the same thing."

"I want you to know that, while I have no intention of either suggesting you end the relationship or allowing my mother to take her frustration out on your father, I still caution you that the duchess may, then, make Darrow the target of her ire."

"Understood."

"I'm going to ask a question that you don't have to answer."

"Go on, then."

"How serious are the two of you?"

Pinch turned his head and looked out the window.

I waited. I'd told Pinch he didn't have to answer, and perhaps he wouldn't.

When he hesitated, I guessed he was struggling with what to say.

"It's very new, Shiv. I care about her. I always have…"

"I sense there's more."

Pinch chuckled. "You know your sister."

"Tell me what's concerning you besides the duchess."

"You cannot share this with Darrow."

"Never."

"I have wondered whether the allure of the forbidden is playing a bigger role between us than it should."

I nodded. If Pinch's instincts were telling him that was the case, then he was likely right, at least partially.

"Can you give me the rundown of what your plan is after we land?" Pinch asked.

I welcomed the change of subject.

"We're flying into Los Angeles where we'll rent separate cars and drive to the Central Coast." I'd received an update from Merrigan saying that Burns Butler had taken the women to Butler Ranch rather than having them drive south to Montecito and risk being inter-cepted on the way.

I'd also heard from Rivet, who told me he was back from Germany and had made contact with United Russia. They denied any involvement, citing the deal they'd made just last November. Given UR stood to lose over a billion dollars if SIS and the CIA suggested their governments issue sanctions, it did seem unlikely that they would pull a stunt like planting the bomb.

Besides, what reason would they have to go after either Losha or Zary at this point? The two had quietly left UR's employ and were making a life for them-selves that didn't involve the intelligence community.

However, if it wasn't UR, who would've planted the bomb? Unfortunately, I couldn't narrow the suspects to a short list. The possibilities were endless.

"What of the bomb?" asked Pinch.

"It was successfully diffused, although it had been scheduled to detonate at three in the morning, not trig-gered by Losha's entry to the house or the basement."

"There would be a signature, then."

"Perhaps, although anyone can gain knowledge to build a bomb from the internet." I was in great favor of regulation of the medium, however far-fetched that notion might be.

"What comes next?"

That was dependent on how much control Losha would relinquish to me. My intention was to take her and the baby somewhere I believed they'd be safe while both the CIA and SIS tried to figure out who had planted the bomb.

The plan was relatively simple; however, the notion of Losha blindly going along with what I wanted was even less likely than an internet regulation.

"Any word on the K19 team?"

"None."

"Protection is in place, though, no?"

"Few better than Burns."

"I've heard he's a legend."

"What's more is that in Burns' case, the stories haven't been exaggerated."

Pinch and I spent the next hour sharing what we'd heard about the former CIA agent who had yet to have an equal in making an op look as though it had never happened.

As far as the technology of intelligence, even SIS had consulted with Burns. And it wasn't just Doc's father who had been a CIA rock star; his mother, Sorcha, was a former operative and medic responsible in part for bringing an end to a decades-long war between United Russia and their nemesis organization, the Maskhadovs.

"Talk about a pedigree," commented Pinch.

"Very true. What's most shocking is that Doc has five other siblings who believed their parents were merely vineyard owners and winemakers. Most of them followed in those footsteps. Only Doc went into intelligence."

"I hope I get to meet Burns and Sorcha."

I smiled. "Oh, you will."

Since Zary had called about the bomb, I'd been without sleep for twenty-four hours straight. If Losha and I turned around and left the States like I wanted to, it would be another twenty before I could rest.

My anxiety over seeing Losha had built on the four-hour drive from the airport to Butler Ranch to the point where I'd considered stopping for a drink. Bad form along with a chicken-shit move for someone who had faced many of the most evil bastards who'd ever walked the face of the earth.

On the surface, it was seeing her, but the deeper issue was getting her to agree to my plan. Maybe I was overthinking it, though. If she saw as clearly as I did that this would be best for her and Kazmir's safety, maybe she'd go along with it willingly.

It was after ten at night when I pulled up and waited for the gates to Butler Ranch to open. I took a deep breath and drove through slowly, stopping at the main house as Burns had asked me to do.

Two things caught my eye straightaway. First was Burns sitting on the front porch, illuminated by the glow of his pipe. Second was the hurried movement of another figure closer to the smaller cottages.

I cut the engine and climbed out of the car.

"She won't get far," Burns said in a tone of voice not much above a whisper, motioning with his head toward the person I'd seen.

"What is she trying to do?"

"Best guess is to find a way off the ranch."

I shook my head. In terms of stealth reconnaissance, my strengths far exceeded Losha's. I'd been given the code name "Shiver" for a reason. I moved through the night air without so much as stirring it, coming up behind her like a ghost.

"I knew you were here," she said when I covered her mouth with one hand while the other wrapped around both her arms.

I spun her around. "What are you doing, Losha?"

"I doubt you'd buy it if I said I was taking a walk."

"Where is Kazmir?"

"Asleep down the hall from Zary." She also pointed to something attached to the waist of her trousers. "Baby monitor."

"A fact-finding mission, then?"

When she tried to pull away, I tightened my grasp.

"Let me go, Shiv," she muttered while, at the same time, relaxing into my embrace.

"Shall we go inside?" I asked.

She traipsed away with a huff that made me smile. If she really hadn't wanted to be discovered, she could've tried a whole lot harder not to be. She knew it as well as I did.

"Ladies first," I said when she opened the door to the cottage.

She shuffled past, trying her hardest not to touch me, but I wouldn't let her get away with it. Instead, I grasped her arm.

"I'm glad you're safe, Losha." I leaned forward and kissed her forehead. "I'd die if anything happened to you."

She pulled away and rounded the corner to the drawing room. "That's where we differ, Shiver. I'd die if anything happened to my son."

"I feel the same way about both of you, Losha."

"How is that possible, Shiver? How could you feel that way about another man's child?"

"Is he?"

She nodded.

"Would you swear it so?"

When she turned her back, I approached again, wrapping my arm around her waist once more, my breath hot just beneath her ear. "Let's not talk about that right now. Let's talk about how to keep both you and the baby safe."

When she tried to pull away again, I let her go.

"I'm perfectly capable of keeping my baby safe. My mistake was in coming here and trusting that anyone else could as well as I."

"Someday you'll have to trust that I would do anything for you, Losha, including giving my own life for yours."

Her eyes met mine.

"I mean it. My life for yours. No hesitation."

"Shiver…"

"It isn't just me. Zary, Gunner, and the rest of the K19 crew, Burns and Sorcha would all do everything in their power to protect you and Kazmir."

She sighed, and I could see her walls lowering, but only slightly.

"I need to disappear, Shiver. You have to let me."

I led her to the sofa and pulled her down to sit beside me. "I have a plan that I'd like you to at least listen to."

"You don't understand. It isn't just me and Kazmir. I put Zary, Gunner, and their unborn baby in harm's way."

"I understand that you're looking at it that way now, but let's talk this through."

"I don't need to talk. I need to leave."

"Let's leave together, then."

"I can't."

I cupped her cheek with my palm. "Hear me out."

She didn't pull away, so I kept talking. "If we go to London, you and Kazmir would have the full protection of SIS."

"In exchange for what?"

"Nothing."

She smirked. "Since when does SIS care about a former Russian assassin, Shiv?"

"It was attempted murder, Losha."

"I reiterate. Why do they care?"

"Primarily because of your relationship with me."

"We don't have a relationship."

"Stop this. I'm not going to relent."

"If he did let up on you, I wouldn't," said Zary from the room's entryway. "You're being ridiculous and worse—prideful. Let him help you, Losha. Let him help Kazmir too."

Losha's cheeks turned pink.

"Let go, Losha," I whispered. "Let me help you and your son." I'd been so tempted to say "our" instead of "your," but I still wasn't one hundred percent convinced Gunner and Zary's theory that the baby was mine was accurate.

"I won't leave Zary until Gunner is back," Losha said, looking between me and her friend.

"That isn't necessary," Zary protested.

"I won't."

"We don't have to. We can stay here or in town until he returns," I offered.

"I'd rather not move Kazmir."

"Not a problem."

She stood with her arms folded. "Good night, then."

I stood too. "Good night."

She walked toward the front door, but I didn't move. I caught the smirk on Zary's face out of the corner of my eye.

"Can I bring you a pillow and blanket?" Zary asked.

"If you would, please," I answered, toeing off my shoes and sitting back down on the sofa.

"You can't stay here," said Losha, again looking between me and Zary.

"He just flew here from London, Losha. Have a heart."

We were all spared further argument when we heard Kazmir's cry through the baby monitor. Losha ran up the stairs, mumbling in Russian as she went.

"If the reason we're all here wasn't so horrifying, I'd be tempted to laugh. She's trying so hard to resist you."

I shook my head. "This too shall pass."

"What will pass, Shiver? The danger, or Losha's stubbornness where you're concerned."

"Both, I hope," I muttered.

"I'll be back with your bedding since I doubt you'll want to sleep in one of the bedrooms upstairs."

"How many ways in and out of here?"

"Just the front door and the kitchen that I've seen, although I haven't checked the basement. Burns did say it's all wired."

I walked through the main level of the house, checking the kitchen door she'd mentioned as well as all the windows. I armed the alarm for "stay" and thanked Zary when she handed me a blanket and pillow.

"She loves you. You know that, right?"

"So everyone keeps telling me."

Zary went back up the stairs.

"Everyone but her," I muttered once she was gone.

22

Losha

I so wanted to slam the bedroom door. If it wouldn't have startled Kazmir, or told Shiver he had the upper hand, I would've.

What had I expected? I'd known Shiver was on his way; I'd even seen the car pull in. Who else would have been arriving at that hour? It wasn't like I'd figured out a plan to leave yet, or that I honestly believed I'd be successful in doing so. Besides, the situation I was in was of my own making.

I'd known asking Zary for help meant that Shiver would find me. Even if Gunner had kept his promise not to tell anyone I was with them or about Kazmir, the smallest intelligence organization of a third world country would've been able to find me easily. And that made the bomb more curious.

If United Russia was tracking me, they could've located me long ago. Why wait until I was in the States and then plant a bomb? Why not simply have a sniper take me out? There had to be something I was missing.

"Knock, knock," I heard Zary say from the other side of the door.

"Come in," I said, although if I hadn't, I doubted it would've stopped my friend from entering.

Zary sat on the edge of the bed that was closest to the chair where I sat nursing Kazmir back to sleep.

"I don't get it. He loves you so much."

"Thanks."

"That isn't what I meant. It's you I don't get."

I looked into Zary's eyes. "Gunner swept you off your feet, and you never looked back. That's how it went, right?"

Zary half smiled. "You're right. I resisted letting him into my life fully even though, in my heart, it was what I wanted. But this is different, Losha. I hadn't had his baby."

I wasn't surprised by Zary's confrontational tone. Neither of us had ever held back where the other was concerned. If one of us believed the other was making a mistake, we didn't hesitate to say so. Just because we hadn't seen each other in several months didn't mean that had changed.

"What are you going to do?"

"Shiver wants us to leave with him."

"And?"

"Have you heard from Gunner?"

"Oh! That's why I came to find you in the first place. He thinks he'll be here by tomorrow night, but he's trying his best to arrive sooner. He was vague, but I sense there's some other part of their mission that hasn't been finalized."

There had been a time when my curiosity would've caused me to at least speculate on K19's mission. Now, I couldn't muster enough enthusiasm to care beyond when Gunner would be here, and that was solely for Zary's sake.

Zary stood. "Get some sleep, Losha. Tomorrow, try to remember what Sorcha said and consider that Shiver would do anything in the world for you."

I was torn between sticking my tongue out and flipping my friend off. Both childish acts were indicative of my level of exhaustion, both physically and mentally.

My mind could compartmentalize all of the things causing my stress, but that didn't mean my body could shut off or alter the effects of the adrenaline that had surged through it. Between the bomb itself and Shiver's arrival, along with my uncertainty about my life and the direction it was going in, I felt unable to act.

Instead of putting Kazmir back in his crib, I snuggled him in the crook of my arm, telling myself we'd just lie together that way for a few minutes.

I hadn't been asleep long, or at least I didn't think I had, when I heard the creak of the door.

"It's me, Losha." Shiver walked in and sat on the side of the bed. "I could hear you whimpering from downstairs." He reached for the lamp on the bedside table and turned it on. "Were you having a bad dream?"

I had been, but I couldn't tell him what about, other than someone was trying to take my baby. I hadn't realized I was crying until he wiped away a tear with his finger.

I looked down at Kazmir and saw his eyes were open. He was studying the man sitting next to us. Shiver leaned over and kissed his forehead and then did the same to me. When he went to stand, I put my hand on his arm.

"Would you like me to stay?" he asked, motioning to the chair near the bed.

I shook my head but kept my hand on his arm.

"Tell me what you want, Losha."

I closed my eyes, wondering again why it was so hard to tell him how I felt. At the same time, I wished he wouldn't force me to. "Stay," I whispered.

When Shiver came around the other side of the bed and lay down, Kazmir smiled at him.

"You make him happy."

"Just him?"

I sighed. "Shiver—"

"Please disregard—"

I sat up. "Why won't you let me finish? I'm trying to tell you what you want to hear, yet you won't let me finish."

Shiver sat up too and pulled Kazmir into his arms. I hated to admit that my baby appeared frightened by my tone.

"I'm sorry," he said. "Please go ahead."

I put my face in my hands. "Zary asked me why it's so hard for me to accept your help, and I told her that I can't explain it. And, yes, Shiver, having you here with me does make me happy. Are you pleased with yourself that you got me to say it?"

He held the baby so close, his cheek resting against Kazmir's head. He rocked back and forth, just slightly, looking as though he was soothing himself as much as my son.

"This isn't a battle, Losha," he said in a soft voice. "I'm not trying to 'get you' to say anything."

I looked up at the ceiling. "I'm sorry," I muttered, wishing I didn't react to him as strongly as I did. Not just in anger, but in everything.

"I heard you whimper, and I came up to see if you were okay, because I care about you." He shrugged. "I don't know why I feel this need to protect you, I just do. It isn't something I'm going to continue apologizing for. You know how I feel. I haven't kept it a secret."

I got out of bed and walked over to the window. "It isn't easy for me." I looked back at him and saw he was waiting for me to continue. "I don't want it to be this hard."

"Neither do I."

"I don't know any other way."

"Sure you do," he said, bringing Kazmir over to me. "It isn't hard for you to love your son."

I took the baby in my arms. "I'm going to put him in the crib in the other room. I'll be right back."

My reasons for doing so were two-fold. First, Kazmir needed sleep, and if Shiver and I kept talking, he wouldn't get it. Second, the distraction of seeing Shiver hold his son was almost too much for me to bear. I'd nearly come to tears several times in the last few minutes.

Maybe Zary was right. I should tell him the truth, both about the baby and how I felt about him, and also give in and let him help and protect me.

Once Kazmir was settled, I went back into the bedroom, but Shiver wasn't there. I went downstairs, looking for him, but he wasn't there either.

23

Shiver

"I'm sorry if I woke you," said Rivet when I returned his call from only a minute ago.

"You didn't. Do you have news?"

"I've spoken with the bomb expert the CIA sent out, as well as Pimm, and neither believe United Russia had anything to do with it."

I didn't know the person the CIA sent, but I knew Pimm, and there was no one with greater knowledge on the subject, particularly as it related to UR.

"Has he come up with another theory?"

"It appears almost random in nature, but before you argue with me, I agree that it wasn't. However, whoever or whatever organization is behind this doesn't seem to possess a great deal of knowledge or money."

"What do you suggest the next move be?"

"While Pimm continues researching the materials used, I recommend you and Ms. Kuznetsov return to the UK immediately. There's a safe house outside of London—"

"She'll be returning to Whittaker Abbey with me."

"I wouldn't recommend that course of action."

"I respectfully decline your suggestion otherwise."

"Very well, but—"

"Are you aware of the child, Ranald?"

"I am, Thornton."

"There is a chance he's mine."

"Understood."

As much as I knew I should go back inside and resume the conversation Losha and I had been having, I was far too wound up to do so.

I wasn't surprised that United Russia hadn't taken responsibility, nor that there wasn't any proof they were behind it. If they had been, the outcome would've been far simpler. Sanctions would be threatened, among other things, and I could ensure that, from that day on, Orina Kuznetsov would be off-limits.

Instead, with no lead on who it was, I felt powerless. How could I tell Losha so? How could I promise to protect her and Kazmir when I didn't know from whom?

Rather than going back inside, I walked the vineyards by moonlight, trying to piece together who, besides her former employer, might want her dead.

The list was far too long—essentially anyone who knew someone she'd killed.

"What brings you out at dawn?" asked Burns, coming over the ridge where I was watching the sunrise.

"I've been out here since a little after midnight, trying to piece together who might've planted the bomb. As I'm sure you know by now, no one believes UR had anything to do with it."

Burns nodded.

"There are too many other suspects to list."

"Could be just about anyone." Burns tapped his pipe on the fence, filled it from his tobacco pouch, and lit it.

"Losha and Raketa have amassed enemies," I said, using the names most in the intelligence community knew them by.

"What do you intend to do next?"

"Take her and Kazmir to Bedfordshire."

"Good decision."

"Rivet didn't think so."

"He and I haven't always agreed either." Burns shook his head and laughed.

"I'd forgotten you and he worked together."

"Not much different than you and Kade."

He made a good point. Burns Butler and Rivet Caird had served side-by-side at a similar age to Doc and me. They were likely as good of friends as well.

"Do you know why Ranald was in Germany?"

I lifted my head. "I don't other than he was on holiday."

"Anna's family is from Kaiserslautern."

I hadn't known that either, but also had no idea what point Burns was trying to make.

"He took her home to say goodbye."

"I wasn't aware she was ill," I answered, looking at the sunrise.

"Rivet is a very private man."

"It's why he's been so desperate for my answer."

"Likely true."

"How bad is she?"

"Terminal. Doubtful she'll live through the month."

Jesus. Here, Rivet was dealing with his wife's illness, and I'd been so wrapped up in trying to find Losha, I hadn't even noticed.

"Go back to England, Thornton. Take Losha and the baby with you. Do what you need to do, and let others do their jobs."

"Understood, sir." I ran my hand through my hair. "She doesn't want to leave Zary until Gunner is back."

"He'll be here tonight," said Burns, relighting his pipe.

"I thought…" I didn't bother finishing my sentence. There was no point in questioning Burns. If he said Gunner would be arriving tonight, he would be.

"I'll start making arrangements."

"After breakfast," Burns muttered. "Sorcha will not be happy if you miss it."

When I walked up to the cottage, I saw Losha sitting outside with Kazmir on her lap.

"What's happened?" she asked.

"Gunner will be back tonight."

"What else? Any word on who planted the bomb?"

"Nothing definitive yet." I sat next to her. "I spoke with both Rivet and Burns. They agree we should return to England. I'm sorry I disappeared on you. Rivet's call…"

"Do they think it was United Russia?"

I shook my head. "As I said, nothing definitive."

"Are we leaving today?"

"I was thinking tomorrow morning."

She stood and turned to go inside.

"Losha?"

She didn't turn back around, but she did stop.

"If you'd rather not return to England with me, I'll do everything in my power to ensure that you and the baby are protected."

"We'll go with you, Shiver," she said before going inside and closing the door behind her.

"There you are," said Sorcha, wiping her hands on a towel and walking over to hug me when I walked into her kitchen.

"I've missed you, Mrs. Butler."

"It's Sorcha as you know well. How are you, Thornton?"

I smiled at her use of my given name like Burns had a short time ago. Other than my mother and sister, almost no one ever used it. Even I thought of myself as Shiver. "I'm well, and you?"

"Come with me," she said, taking my hand and pulling me through the kitchen and out the door to the back porch.

"I was sorry to hear about your father's passing."

"I appreciate it."

She sat on the porch swing and patted the seat beside her; I sat too.

"Let's talk about Losha and that precious baby."

"Of course." I was anxious to hear what she had to say.

"She's struggling. She wants to trust you, but her instincts are telling her she can trust no one."

"Did she admit this?"

Sorcha laughed. "Of course she didn't, but, Thornton, you must never give her cause to doubt you. Earn her trust and prove to her she'll always have your support."

"What if she doesn't want it?"

"Oh, she does. More than anything."

I followed her back into the house. "Can I help?" I asked, looking at the mess in the kitchen.

"Here," she said, pointing to a pan and handing me a slab of bacon.

When that and the pancakes Sorcha made were ready, I helped her carry the heaping platters into the dining room.

The first face I saw was Losha's, smiling at something Burns had said. I loved her smile, and her laugh, and everything about the woman. What would it take to get her to love me back?

24

Losha

I was listening to Burns, but looked up when Shiver came in from the kitchen. Sorcha was barking instructions at him, but his eyes were focused on mine.

He had the most beautiful eyes, and sometimes I felt that he could see straight into my soul. The way he'd always looked at me made me feel cherished, something I didn't remember ever feeling, even from my parents.

He set the platters of food where Sorcha told him to, walked over to where I sat, and leaned down to whisper in my ear. "I'd love to know what you're thinking about right now."

"You."

Shiver looked into my eyes. "What about me?"

I smiled. "Maybe I'll tell you later."

"Hello? Where is everyone?" I heard someone say from the direction of the front door.

"Kade!" Sorcha squealed, which made Kazmir squeal too and everyone else laugh.

The woman greeted her oldest son, followed by Burns, and then Shiver. It was obvious the two were close, more than I'd realized.

I'd heard as many stories about "Doc" Butler as I had about his father, but I'd never met him.

Kade walked back outside and held the door open for a woman I had also heard of but never met. Merrigan "Fatale" Shaw-Butler was as infamous as her husband. Maybe more so.

The first I'd heard her name was from another KGB assassin, Sergei *"Oruzhiye"* Orlov. Known in the intelligence community as "the gun," Orlov had trained both Zary and me.

Like most of the people in our world, there were two sides to Sergei—the cold, hard killer and the sweet man no one believed could harm a fly.

He'd admitted once, after several shots of vodka, that he'd been in love with Fatale Shaw, but she didn't return the affection. Those were his words, and to this day, I remembered how heartbroken he'd looked when he spoke them.

"Losha." Shiver approached with both Doc and his wife. "I'd like you to meet two of my closest friends."

I stood and shook both of their hands. "Who is this?" I asked, holding my finger out to the baby in Merrigan's arms.

"This is Laird"—the woman beamed—"who is getting very heavy." Merrigan handed the baby to his father.

"I knew a friend of yours," I said once Doc and Shiver had walked away.

Merrigan raised a brow and took off her coat.

"Sergei," I whispered.

The woman scrunched her eyes. "An enigma, that man. I can't decide whether the world is blessed by his passing or if he somehow might've redeemed himself."

I leaned in. "I've heard he's still alive."

Merrigan nodded. "Until yesterday."

"Oh!" I gasped, causing everyone in the room to look our way. "I agree with your assessment," I said once those in the room lost interest in what we were discussing. "Like others who do what we do, I'm sure there are many who consider us evil."

Merrigan put her arm around my shoulders. "Many do not. Come introduce me to your baby boy."

"This is Kazmir," I said, lifting him out of Zary's arms.

"It's good to see you," said Merrigan when Zary stood to hug her. "How are you holding up?"

"I miss Gunner, but otherwise, okay."

As soon as she'd spoken his name, the front door opened again and Gunner walked through it. When Zary flew across the room and into his arms, my eyes filled with tears at seeing my friend's unabashed happiness.

"I can't say I would've predicted I'd ever see that look on Gunner's face, but there it is," said Shiver, who came to stand next to me.

Kazmir reached his little arms out, and I passed him to Shiver.

"You don't mind, do you?" he asked.

"Not at all. I was going to ask you the same thing."

"Never. I'll hold him as often as you'll let me."

My eyes focused on his. Would he? What about when the baby was fussy or needed a diaper change? Something told me he would still want to hold him. Could the Shiver standing before me, nuzzling my baby, be real?

"There it is again."

"What's that?"

"The look you promised to tell me about later."

I smiled. "He's hungry," I added when Kazmir rubbed his face on Shiver's chest. He was teething and left a trail of drool wherever he rubbed. "I'm sorry about your shirt." I took Kazmir from his arms and handed him a cloth. "I should've given you this when you took him."

He looked down at his perfectly pressed button-down shirt and smiled. "I don't mind in the least."

When I walked down the hall to the room Sorcha told me I could use to nurse the baby, Shiver followed. "What do you need?" I asked.

"You, would be my first answer. After that, to watch you with your son, even if only for the minute you'll let me."

"Why do you think I'd only allow you a minute?"

"Does it bother you?"

"That you want to watch me nurse him? No, oddly it doesn't."

"Thank you, Losha."

"Don't thank me. Listen, Shiv—"

"Hey, where the hell did you go?" Gunner shouted from the hallway at the same time I spoke.

"Here," Shiver answered and then leaned forward to kiss my cheek. "I'll be back in a minute."

Once again, at the same moment I'd decided to tell him he was Kazmir's father, he was called away. I couldn't help but think the universe was trying to tell me not to.

"What do you think, baby boy? Should we tell him he's your daddy?" I whispered.

Kazmir brought two fingers to his mouth and started to cry.

"Guess not," I said to myself after getting the baby settled on my breast.

25

Shiver

Something told me that leaving the room when I had was a mistake. What was Losha about to say when Gunner called out my name?

I followed him out the same kitchen door I'd followed Sorcha through a couple of hours ago. "What's going on?" I asked when I saw Doc and Pinch waiting.

"Brief me on what you know about the bomb," said Doc.

Pinch told him what we'd learned from both Pimm and the bomb expert the CIA had sent out. However, it wasn't much. At this point, all we knew was who hadn't planted it, but had no theories as to who had.

"What's your plan?" Gunner asked.

"We're leaving for Bedfordshire tonight," I told them. "Originally, I'd planned for tomorrow, but since you're back early…"

Both Doc and Gunner nodded.

"Let me know what the K19 team can do to help," said Doc, resting his hand on my shoulder.

"Keep your ears open. Let me know of anything you hear, even if it seems incredible."

"If you need more feet on the ground, let us know," Gunner added.

"Appreciate it." I looked between the three men. "Anything else?"

When they all shook their heads, I went back inside, hoping I could salvage the moment with Losha. Instead, I found both her and Kazmir sound asleep.

I eased the door closed and went back out to where the Butler family and friends were gathered.

After dinner, I loaded the rental car with the items Sorcha insisted we take with us for the baby, and wondered again if I was doing the wrong thing by taking them to Bedfordshire. When I'd told Losha I thought we should leave tonight, her reaction had been…resigned.

"We'll go with you, Shiver," she'd said earlier, as though if she'd had another choice, she wouldn't have.

I walked up the steps of the porch and into the house, where I found her still sitting at the big farmhouse table. Sorcha held Kazmir on her lap while Burns played peek-a-boo with the baby. Peals of laughter from both Kazmir and his mother pulled at my heartstrings.

Would they be happier staying here with the Butlers? The family would certainly welcome them.

"Must you go so soon?" I heard Sorcha ask, realizing she was directing her question at me.

"I'm afraid we do."

"But the bairn—"

"Now, Sorcha," said Burns. "We discussed this at great length. It's for the wee boy's and his mother's safety that they must return to London."

"Nach bhfuil acu a."

"Yes, they do," Burns reiterated, smiling at his wife, who mumbled something more in Gaelic that I didn't catch.

"Ready?" I asked Losha.

"Zary?"

"She and Gunner are out front."

"I'll say my goodbyes, then."

When I walked closer to Sorcha, Kazmir held his hands out to be picked up. I looked at Losha, who nodded, before I took the baby in my arms.

"Do you have everything I told you to take?" Sorcha asked.

"I didn't leave anything behind," I answered before Burns could chide her for nagging, and carried the baby outside. I nuzzled Kazmir's neck, which made him coo, and marveled at how natural it felt to hold him when I doubted I'd been around a baby since shortly after my sister was born.

"We're off," I said to Gunner, who met me on the porch.

3:24 "Godspeed, and again, let us know if there's anything we can do to help."

"Thanks, mate."

Pinch came out, smiling and shaking Doc's and Burns' hands and hugging Sorcha. "Thanks for having me," he said. "I wish we didn't have to leave so soon."

I looked over at Losha and Zary, both of them in tears, and wondered again if I was making a terrible mistake.

26

Losha

"You're doing the right thing, Losha," said Zary. "I'm proud of you for not fighting Shiver on this."

"I have little choice."

Zary scrunched her eyes and put her hand on her hip. "Of course you do. You could stay here. I'm sure both Sorcha and Burns would love to have you and Kazmir stay indefinitely. You could also stay with Gunner and me. There is no way anyone will be gaining access to the duplex ever again."

I'd heard Burns talking to Shiver about that very thing. There was a team already working on fixing the holes in the beach house's security system while other teams were analyzing the systems in place at several of the other houses owned by K19 Security Solutions' partners—Butler Ranch included.

Kazmir and I would be very safe if we stayed, but I'd still be jeopardizing the safety of everyone who lived here.

"Let Shiver take care of you and the baby," Zary said through her tears.

"Ready?" Shiver asked, walking up behind me.

"Sure."

He handed Kazmir to me and then opened the back passenger door. I bent down to put the baby in the car seat, when I felt Shiver's hand on my shoulder.

"Wait," I heard him say, and turned back around, straightening to look at him.

"What?"

"We don't have to do this. If you really don't want to go to London, I won't force you."

"It's fine. I understand it's for the best."

When he nodded, I went back to securing Kazmir in the car seat.

"I'll see you in July, if not sooner," Zary said when I walked around the car to get in the front passenger seat.

"July?" asked Shiver.

"Our wedding," Zary told him. "We can't be married without my maid of honor."

Before I dissolved into tears a second time, I got in the car. Would I be back in July? Or would doing so bring danger back to Zary, Gunner, and their baby? Only time would tell.

Both Shiver and I were quiet on the drive to the airfield in San Luis Obispo. He'd told me a private jet was waiting to take us from there to Los Angeles, where we'd take a different private aircraft to London. SIS clearly had a great deal more money than United Russia, given the way we were traveling. On the other hand, Shiver was a duke now. Perhaps the jets belonged to him.

"Pinch should be here shortly, and then we'll leave."

Part of me had hoped that Shiver and I would have some time alone on the trip so we could talk things through. I'd decided only a few short hours ago not to keep the fact that he was Kazmir's father from him any longer. Except, every time I tried to tell him, I was interrupted. Perhaps it would be better to wait until we landed in London and I could speak with him privately without fear of another interruption.

"Pinch is the one who found me in Lapland."

"I'm sorry, Losha."

"Why?"

"I had to know where you were. I had to know you were safe."

"I know," I whispered, looking out the car window at the vast expanse of the Pacific Ocean.

All too soon, we arrived at the airfield where Kazmir and I were whisked onto the small plane.

"The next one will be far more comfortable," Shiver said as he helped get Kazmir settled into the car seat that we'd strapped to a seat on the plane. "We'll only be in the air an hour."

I closed my eyes and feigned sleep when I heard Pinch board.

Shiver hadn't exaggerated about how much nicer the plane was that we took from Los Angeles to London. Once we were in the air, at cruising altitude, he led Kazmir and me to the back.

"There are two staterooms. You can lie down if you'd like," he said while setting up the portable crib for the baby.

"Shiver, this is…"

He stopped what he was doing and met my gaze.

"Thank you. I appreciate what you're doing very much."

"You're welcome," he murmured, giving me the sense that he wasn't looking for my thanks but something else entirely.

With hooded eyes, he left me alone to contemplate why I found it so hard to share my feelings with him.

I heard the door open and rolled to my back.

"Good afternoon, my sleeping beauties," said Shiver, bending at the waist to lift Kazmir out of the crib. The baby kicked his legs and babbled at him, putting his tiny hand on his cheek.

"He likes you."

"He has good taste."

As soon as he spoke, Kazmir got fussy and reached out for me.

"Don't take it personally," I said when I saw his face fall. "He's hungry."

"I came back to see if you needed anything."

I lifted my shirt, unfastened the cup of the maternity bra, and let Kazmir get settled before I looked up at him. "I don't think so, but thank you."

"I apologize for staring. You're both just so beautiful."

I felt my cheeks heat. "Thank you," I repeated.

"I'll go back out, then," he said, but didn't move.

"You can stay."

"I shouldn't. I...uh..."

"Are you okay?" I asked.

"Pardon? I mean, yes, I'm fine..."

"Shiver?"

"I'll be back later," he said and walked out.

I tilted my head and looked at my sweet son, nursing happily while a war waged inside me.

Things had never been easy between Shiver and me. At first it was all about undeniable attraction. It still was to a certain extent. The sound of his voice alone made me long to feel his naked body against mine.

***

"I've heard about you," I said to the man who had come up behind where I sat at the bar, without making a sound.

"What have you heard?" he asked, his mouth so close to my neck that I could feel the heat of his breath.

"You make women shiver."

"What about you? Do I make you shiver?"

With his mouth still so close to my neck, I leaned into him so his lips almost made contact with my skin.

"Tell me, Orina, do I?" he said in an English accent that had to be part of his charm.

"How do you know my name?" I asked, closing my eyes and wishing I could feel his naked body against mine.

"I asked around."

"Why?"

"You are the most captivating woman I've ever seen."

"Is that all?"

"Isn't that enough?"

"It has nothing to do with whom I work for?" I signaled the bartender, who poured another shot of icy-cold vodka. "One for the gentleman, please."

When Shiver reached around me to pick up the shot glass, he rubbed against me.

"In spite of it," he said.

"Za zdorovje." I raised my glass.

"To your health," he answered, waiting until I brought the glass to my lips before he did. When he sat on the barstool next to me, I missed the warmth of his body so close to mine.

"You are handsome as well as charming," I said, looking into his green-gray eyes, wondering if he looked as good out of clothes as he did in them. Probably better, I decided as I took him in, starting with his alluring eyes to his chin, covered with just the right amount of stubble. His hair was dark, thick, and wavy, but shaved on the sides.

His perfectly pressed white dress shirt was open at the neck, revealing skin that was tan from time in the sun, and the dark-blue suit jacket he wore was snug on his muscular arms.

His long, thick fingers hinted at the power and breadth of other parts of his body. His legs, too, strained against his custom-cut, dark-blue trousers. The man had to be rock solid underneath all the fabric.

"Well? What do you think?" he asked, his chin resting against his fist.

"You are the most captivating man I've ever seen."

Shiver leaned forward so his lips were once again just below my ear.

"I'd say, then, we're the perfect match."

"Only one problem," I said, moving away from him.

He smirked, leaning back into his fist. "I can't wait to hear it."

"How do you know I'm not here to kill you?"

"I cannot imagine a more exquisite way to go."

***

When Kazmir fussed, I moved him to the opposite breast and then leaned back against the pillow, closing my eyes and willing the memory of the first time I met Thornton "Shiver" Whittaker to come back into focus.

27

Shiver

I tried my damnedest to focus on my conversation with Pinch, but when I as much as blinked, the image of Losha with the baby at her breast was all I could see.

How lucky were women that they had the ability not only to feel a child growing inside them, but to bring them to life, and then feed and nurture them with nothing but their own body?

Just looking at the two of them brought my primal need to protect the baby and his mother to the surface. I couldn't imagine how intense that feeling would be in her.

I didn't need her to explain to me that she'd die protecting Kazmir; as I'd told her, I would do the same.

"Shiv?"

"Right. Sorry."

"We'll talk later," said Pinch.

"Bloody good idea." I stood and went to the back of the plane. As much as I wanted to join Losha and the baby, I opened the opposite door instead and lay on the bed.

Exhaustion overwhelmed me, and I let my eyes drift closed. For the time being, she and Kazmir were safe, and I could allow myself to rest.

How long had I loved her? Maybe from the first night we met.

***

I could only see the woman's long dark hair, but I knew it was Orina "Losha" Kuznetsov sitting at the bar alone. It was a known hangout for the military intelligence set, which made the Russian assassin's presence at a bar across the way from SIS headquarters all the more intriguing. She was on my turf, and I wondered why.

As I approached, her scent wafted over me, almost pulling me into her. I got close enough to touch, but didn't. Instead, I breathed her in, willing my memory to commit her every last detail.

As we talked, I found her verbal sparring turned me on as much as her beauty—maybe more. Her eyes sparkled as she challenged me with her sexy-as-bloody-hell Russian accent.

It was rare to the point of being unheard of that I reacted to a woman so strongly that my only thought was of stripping her out of the black sheath she wore and spending hours learning every inch of the body beneath.

After our second shot of Russian vodka, she stood and grabbed the lapels of my jacket. I looked straight into her deep-gray almost-black eyes, willing her to bring her lips to mine.

Instead, I felt her tongue on my cheek as she licked from the corner of my mouth up to just below my eye. "You know why I'm here," she whispered.

I took a deep breath, barely able to contain my hardness straining against my zipper.

When she let go and walked away without looking back, I was filled with profound disappointment and a burning need to know why she'd come to that particular bar at that precise time.

***

If I concentrated hard enough, I could recall the scent that had lingered after her that night. Like now, my body yearned for hers with such ferocity that every woman I'd met since did nothing for me—to the point I'd wondered if I should consider monkhood.

The idea, the dream, the cautious hope that my seed was the one that had joined with hers and created the divine angel that was Kazmir, settled in my chest.

Only knowing how crushed I'd be to find out I wasn't his father, kept me from all-out claiming the baby as mine.

What might have happened, I wondered, if Rivet hadn't called two nights ago. Would Losha have come back into the bedroom, stripped out of her clothes, and laid her body next to mine? Would she have run her tongue from my neck to my ear like she loved to do? Would she have let me sink into her warm, wet body? Would she have cried and begged me to go deeper, faster, harder? Would she have fallen apart in my arms, her face flushed with our combined heat, a layer of sweat coating every inch of her skin?

Would she have finally told me she loved me?

And there it was. The wall that stood between us was her inability to talk about her feelings. Beneath that hard shell she kept so firmly in place, I believed she cared about me, even loved me, but Losha couldn't bring herself to say the words.

There'd been a time I believed her incapable of doing so. Not because she didn't have feelings for me, but because her upbringing—being orphaned, being taken and trained by the KGB—had taught her she could never truly trust the love that was given to her enough to freely give it in return.

28

Losha

When the pilot announced we'd land in under an hour, I found myself wishing our time in the sky could last a little longer. What I'd face once we arrived was an abyss of uncertainty.

Where would Shiver take me? How much time would he spend with Kazmir and me? And the worst question of all—who had planted the bomb that almost killed me, my baby, and my pregnant best friend?

Filled with trepidation, I made my way out to the main cabin with Kazmir in my arms.

"May I?" asked Pinch.

"Would you like to hold him?"

"I would."

I handed Pinch the baby and watched as both he and Shiver played with him. Soon they had him in fits of giggles.

What would it be like if this was my life—Shiver and me, raising our son together with the love and laughter of his friends and mine? Right now, it felt like a dream. One that would be ending as soon as the plane landed.

Shiver sat in the seat next to me, and we both watched Pinch continue entertaining Kazmir. "Lost in thought, darling?"

I looked into his eyes. "Darling?"

Shiver smiled. "It's what the duke always called the duchess."

"I'm sorry about your father," I said, reaching for his hand.

"Thank you." He leaned in and kissed my temple. "I miss you so much."

I rested my forehead against his. "I miss you too."

I expected him to pull back, to make me look into his eyes, to ask if that meant I loved him, but he did none of those things. Instead, he didn't even flinch. Not a single muscle moved. It was as though it was the most natural thing in the world for me to say even though I'd never said anything like it before.

Kazmir fussed, and Pinch brought him over to where I sat. Instead of reaching for me, he reached for Shiver. He settled on Shiver's lap, head on his chest, and soon was sound asleep.

"Might have better luck fastening him in while he's asleep," suggested Pinch.

Earlier, when we were getting ready to take off, Kazmir had wanted no part of staying in his car seat, and it wasn't me he'd reached for then either; it had been Shiver.

"He's a sweet nipper," Pinch whispered. "Wait until my father sees him. You'll have a right child watcher with him."

I smiled. How easy this camaraderie was. Apart from my friendship with Zary, I hadn't experienced easy relationships with many people. Shiver was the next closest person I had to a friend.

"Shiv told you SIS doesn't believe UR had anything to do with the bomb?"

The look on Shiver's face said everything I needed to know. This wasn't news to him. He'd known this earlier, when I'd asked him outright. He hadn't told me then, and he hadn't intended to. Instead, he'd lied.

He fastened the latch of the baby seat and slowly approached.

"Don't," I seethed, walking to the single seat next to Kazmir.

"Losha—"

"I said, 'don't.'" I looked out the window, afraid that if I looked at him, I'd cry.

"I'm sorry, I was going to—"

I spun my head and glared at him. "Tell me, Shiver? Was that what you were going to do? Were you going to admit that you lied to me when you finally got around to telling me something that directly impacts my life and the life of my son? Is that what you were going to do?"

I looked back toward the window, relieved when he didn't say anything else. The easy peace that had blossomed between us for the briefest time was now shattered.

Neither Shiver, Pinch, nor I spoke again until we were in the limousine.

"Where are we going?" I asked when it looked like we were leaving London.

"To the abbey," Shiver muttered.

"What did you say?"

He looked straight at me. "We're going to Whittaker Abbey, and that is where you and Kazmir will stay until we've been able to ascertain who planted the bomb and ensure there is no further threat."

"Like hell, we will," I spat back at him. "Driver," I said, opening the partition between us. "Please turn around and take me back to London."

I could see the man's eyes meet Shiver's in the rearview mirror, and saw Shiver shake his head.

"Are you kidnapping us?"

"Losha, please. These antics aren't necessary."

"*Antics?* Did you say antics?"

Even Pinch cringed.

"That isn't what I meant."

"Really? In the same way that you didn't mean it when you told me that they'd found nothing definitive about the bomb?"

"I told you the truth."

"Leaving out the part about United Russia's lack of involvement."

"There was no need to worry you until we knew more. There still isn't."

This time Pinch didn't just cringe; he groaned.

29

Shiver

Losha was livid, and I was ready to throttle Pinch. Why couldn't the man simply keep his bloody mouth shut until we'd reached the abbey?

Once I got Losha and the baby settled, my intention had been to check in with Rivet to see if Pimm had developed a theory yet as to the bomb's maker. Depending on his response, I may or may not have passed on that knowledge to her. I meant what I'd said; until there was more definitive information, there was no need for her to worry or speculate. I was doing enough of that for us both.

When the driver pulled through the gates of Whittaker Abbey, I looked out at the estate that was now, in essence, mine. It looked different somehow, as though I were seeing it through a new set of eyes. For most of my life, the abbey had simply looked like my home. Now, from a distance, I saw it more as it was originally intended. The Palladian-style of architecture, so popular at its time of construction, had been more frequently employed in the design of public and municipal buildings, as the abbey was. Within its central freestanding "temple," there was a main portico and entryway along with the dining rooms, ballroom, kitchen, and library. Two side porticos connected the symmetrical wings of the abbey, which housed the main drawing rooms and bedchambers, many of which were suites.

There was a fine mist hovering over the gardens between the drive and the abbey, giving them an ethereal look. I thought of my mother, who was most likely sitting in her favorite drawing room, oblivious to the fact that, in only a few minutes' time, her life would be irrevocably changed. Whether Kazmir was my baby or not, whether I modified the terms of the trust that had been handed down for generations, whether I accepted Rivet's offer to take over MI6, the duchess would not know what hit her.

Her son, the one she'd plied and molded, guilted into doing her bidding, was no longer. I, Thornton "Shiver" Whittaker, was my own man. I had hard decisions to make, both about my own life and the lives of those I cared about. What my mother wanted or, more importantly, didn't want, no longer mattered unless whatever it was, directly impacted her in a negative way.

"Where to, sir?" asked the driver.

"Pinch?"

"Drop me at Covington House, please."

It was as though Pinch was reading my thoughts. Part of what the duchess would have to accept was Darrow's relationship with the groundskeeper's son— whatever it was, for however long it lasted. I almost smiled in amusement when I imagined her reaction.

I didn't, though. Seated across from me was a very unhappy woman, and her reason for being so rested squarely on my shoulders.

"Where will Kazmir and I be staying?" she asked. They were the first words she'd spoken to me in several minutes.

"The main house for now. We can discuss where you'd be most comfortable, longer term, tomorrow."

She nodded, looking back out the window. "It's beautiful," I thought I heard her whisper.

"That's my favorite of the gardens," said Pinch, pointing to the section where hollyhocks and wild roses grew. "I spent a lot of time in all twenty-eight acres of them, but that one brought me a certain peace."

I looked over at the faraway look on Pinch's face.

"My father and his father before him took great care to preserve the local biodiversity, whether it's with the cutting gardens, the great lawns, or the ponds and woodland areas."

I would've loved to add to what Pinch said, and tell her which were my favorites. I, too, was proud of how my father and grandfathers honored the land and their responsibility to preserve it not only for future generations but also for the monarchy. However, Losha was too angry to listen to me wax nostalgic about my familial heritage. At least, for now, she was speaking to one of us.

The driver pulled up to the residence where Darrow lived, and before I could ask Pinch to tell my sister we'd see her later, she was to the car.

Darrow threw her arms around Pinch, who hugged her too.

"Thank God you're back," she said, trying to see into the car. "Who's that with you?"

Before she could look, my friend put his arm around her shoulders. "We'll see them later," I heard him say before leading her down the path toward the front door of the house.

She beamed back at him, leaving me feeling both happy for my sister and sad for myself. It was unlikely I'd ever be graced with such a gaze from Losha. For the time being, I just hoped she'd talk to me.

"My mother, the duchess…" I began, not knowing what to say next.

It didn't matter; Losha acted as though I hadn't uttered a word.

Kazmir opened his eyes and looked first at me and then at his mother. I expected him to cry or make a fuss about being in the car seat, but he did neither.

"Hello, baby boy." Losha ran her finger down Kazmir's cheek. "I'll get you out in just a minute when the car stops."

The baby studied her and then sat up and looked around, babbling and sucking on the first two fingers of his right hand. It seemed to me that I'd known another baby that had done the same, but I couldn't place who it was. Perhaps all babies did so and thumb-sucking was simply a cliché.

"It's really lovely, Shiver," she said, startling me.

"Pinch's father, Wellie, is our head groundskeeper."

She nodded as though that meant something to her.

"Losha, I'm—"

When she shook her head and I saw the tentative smile leave her face, I stopped talking. There was no point in pushing anything now. Soon, she'd meet the duchess and that, in itself, was going to be daunting for both Losha and me.

"Thornton?" my mother said from her drawing room. "I didn't expect—" The duchess looked between me and Losha and then at the baby. "Who is this?"

"Duchess, I'd like you to meet Orina Kuznetsov and her son, Kazmir."

Losha stepped forward. "It's nice to meet you."

My mother's eyes were wide as she studied the baby in Losha's arms. I expected her to step closer, say hello like most people did when they saw the beautiful little boy. Instead, she stood where she was.

"Why are you here?" she asked, still looking at the baby.

"Mother?"

The name I called her so seldom seemed to jar her out of the trance she'd slipped into. She embraced me when I walked closer to her, but when I pulled away, her eyes went back to the baby.

"Shiver," Losha whispered.

"Yes." I walked the short distance that felt so expansive, creating a gulf between my mother and her.

"I need to change him," she said, again whispering.

"Excuse me," I heard my mother say, and watched as she walked up the stairs. Her behavior was so odd, I didn't know what to make of it.

I showed Losha to the downstairs toilet, realizing that it had no convenient space to change the baby's diaper.

"Come with me." I led her back to the main hallway and over to the stairs.

"No," she said, pulling away. "I'd rather not go up there."

"Why ever not?" I ran my hand through my hair. What on earth was going on between Losha and my mother? I felt as though I was missing something very obvious, but I felt completely in the dark.

"Is there somewhere else I can stay?" she asked, lips trembling and eyes filling with tears.

I had to admit my mother's greeting had been less than welcoming, to the point of being rude.

"Of course," I muttered, trying to figure out which of the residences would make the most sense.

Darrow's Covington House was the first that came to mind, but interrupting her and Pinch would likely feel as awkward as her introduction to the duchess.

"Come with me." I led her back out the front door.

When I saw the limousine had already been parked in the garage, it occurred to me that I hadn't yet taken Kazmir's car seat out of it, nor our bags.

"Bloody hell," I muttered, pulling out my cell phone. "Please bring the car back 'round," I said when the driver answered. "We'll sort out the car seat and bags later," I added after I hung up.

Dorchester House would be the best place for them to stay, but I'd need to discuss that with Wilder first.

Losha nodded as she swayed from side to side and bounced the baby in her arms.

"Is he okay?" I asked.

"Yes. Why?"

"I've never seen you do that with him before."

She immediately stopped, as though she hadn't realized what she was doing.

"I know this is terribly inconvenient," I said, opening the back door to the limo when it pulled up, "but as I said, we'll get everything sorted out later."

She nodded. "Of course."

When we pulled up in front of Wellie's cottage and the old man came out the front door, I felt as though I'd finally stumbled back into the universe as I knew it.

"Who is this wee one?" he asked when I took Kazmir from Losha's arms so she could get out of the car.

"This is Losha," I told him, motioning with my head. "And this is her son, Kazmir. Losha, this is Wellie, surrogate father to all but Pinch, for whom he's the real thing."

"What a sweet little nipper," Wellie said, getting closer and smiling at the baby, who reached out and put his tiny hand near his face. "Oh, I miss the smell of a baby. There's nothing like it on earth, is there?"

Losha laughed. "Right now, he is in desperate need of a diaper change."

"Come in, come in," said Wellie, motioning to his front door. Once inside, he led her down the hallway. "There is a bed where you can change him, and if you need the loo, it's just across the hall."

"Thank you," Losha said before Wellie closed the bedroom door and came back out to join me.

"I'll just let the driver know we won't be needing him straightaway," I said, walking back out front. "I'll transfer Kazmir's seat to the estate car later. You can head back now," I said to the man waiting with the limo. "Tell me your name again?"

"Thomas, and I can do that, sir," he said. "As you know, I have my own wee ones."

"Right. Apologies. And thank you," I mumbled, going back inside.

"I feel daft not remembering a thing about Thomas. He had to remind me he has children of his own."

"Thomas?" asked Wellie.

"The driver."

"I don't know him, so I don't know why you would."

I shrugged. Maybe he was part of the security team Pinch and Rivet had set up. However, that didn't change the fact that as duke, I should know the names of those who worked for me, as well as about their families. It was something my father had always done.

Wellie reached for one of his unmarked bottles. "I reckon you need this right about now," he said, pouring me a shot.

"How did you know?"

"You look as shell-shocked as the blokes who came back from the Great War," he said, pouring me a second shot after I'd downed the first.

"Are you trying to get me pissed?"

Wellie laughed. "I'll serve you no more, but two, you needed." He put the bottle back on the shelf and pulled out a chair. "Have a seat. I'll check on the bonny lass."

I sat, leaned forward, and put my head in my hands.

Wellie came back to the table. "She's almost finished."

"What the bloody hell?" said Wilder, barging through Wellie's door. "Have you forgotten you have a brother, you wanker?"

Other than when Wellie came outside when we first pulled up, I doubted I'd ever felt happier to see someone in recent days. Thank the dear Lord that Wilder's demeanor was as normal as ever.

I put my arms around my brother and patted his back. "We saw the duchess," I said before letting go.

"Losha?"

"And the baby."

Wilder stepped back and scrubbed his face with his hand. "That explains a lot."

"Why? What happened?"

"I saw the duchess come upstairs, but wasn't fast enough to catch her before she went into her chambers and closed the door. She looked as though she'd seen a ghost—and not a friendly one."

"Shh," cautioned Wellie, motioning toward the hallway.

Moments later, Losha came out with the baby in her arms.

"Hello," she said to Wilder. "You must be Shiver's brother."

"His younger and more handsome brother," he answered, smiling and stepping forward to shake her hand and tug on the baby's foot. "Is this Kazmir?"

She nodded and looked at me.

"I've spoken at great length to my brother about the most beautiful baby who has ever lived," I said.

She smiled and her cheeks pinkened. "Isn't he?"

"Right so," said Wellie, coming closer as well.

It dawned on me that all this commotion and strangers getting so close might frighten Kazmir, but he seemed more curious than scared. When he saw my eyes on him, Kazmir reached out.

"Do you mind?" I said to Losha, who tentatively handed him over.

"This is my good friend, Wellie, and that bloke is my brother. His name is Sutton, but we call him Wilder."

Kazmir kept his gaze focused on me and then buried his head, peeking at the two men every few seconds.

"As I remember, it's about this age they get shy," said Wellie, taking a step back. "Please," he said to Losha and pointed to the chair near the fireplace. "Would you like to sit?"

"I would, thank you." She kept her eyes on me and Kazmir, but walked over and sat down. Wilder sat in the opposite chair.

"So you met the duchess?"

She nodded.

"I'm afraid she wasn't very welcoming. I'm sorry about that, Losha."

"She wasn't expecting us, I gather."

No, she hadn't been, and only now did I see the error in the way I'd handled it. I should have forewarned her in some way.

"It was almost as though she'd seen Kazmir before."

"She had," said Wellie. "His likeness anyway."

"What do you mean?" I asked.

Wellie looked first at Losha, who stood, and then at me. "Don't you see it?"

"Get on with it, Wellie," prodded Wilder. "Don't we see what?"

"For goodness' sake, the wee boy is the spitting image of his father."

30

Losha

It was as though everyone in the room froze, except Kazmir, who babbled at the man staring at him like he was seeing him for the very first time.

What must Shiver be thinking? Had he already realized Kazmir was his, but hadn't wanted to admit it? When he turned and looked at me with a tear in his eye, I knew he hadn't.

"I'd hoped," he whispered, walking toward me as though he and I were the only two people in the room, other than our baby.

Out of the corner of my eye, I saw Wellie and Wilder walk out the front door of the cottage and close it behind them.

How I wished I could rewind time and prepare myself better for this moment. I closed my eyes and waited for Shiver's recrimination. I could feel him come close and cup my cheek with his palm.

"Losha, please look at me."

When I opened my eyes, Kazmir leaned forward and touched my opposite cheek with his tiny hand. It was as though they were soothing my worry together—father and son.

"You must have questions," I murmured, looking into Shiver's eyes.

Instead of answering, he leaned closer and touched his lips to mine. From there he kissed each cheek, both of my eyelids, my forehead, and then back to my lips.

"You are so brave," he whispered.

I shook my head. "I'm not," I cried. "I wasn't brave at all."

"You're so wrong. Just look at him. He's perfect. You did that. You kept him safe."

"I was so afraid. I still am."

Shiver drew me close. "I'll keep you safe, Losha. Let me take over now."

"How will you ever forgive me?"

Shiver wiped the tears from my cheeks.

"There is nothing to forgive, my beautiful darling."

I shook my head and took a step backward. "I kept him from you. I lied to you and told you he was another man's child. How can you say there's nothing to forgive?"

"Come," he said, pulling me back to the chair near the fireplace. When I sat, he knelt beside me, Kazmir still in his arms. "Look at me, Losha." He waited until my eyes met his. "The way I see it, you had a good reason not to tell me. In the beginning, there was great danger from United Russia. And then, once the bounty was lifted, you were unsure of whom you could trust."

I couldn't believe he was being as straightforward and levelheaded as he was. I should've known he would be. He always had been. But keeping his son from him—I'd expected him to react differently.

"I only added to your anxiety and fear by relentlessly searching for you. It breaks my heart to think that you and Kazmir had to flee Lapland because Pinch discovered you were living there."

"It brought me to you."

"Yes, but you shouldn't have had to feel as though you were on the run from me when you had so many other things worrying you."

"Shiver…" I shook my head, unsure of what else to say. He was trying to convince *me* that he had no reason to be angry.

He kissed Kazmir's nose, which made him giggle. "He's perfect, Losha. Such a happy baby. You did that.

How could I ever be angry with you for bringing my child into this world?"

"Um…it's kind of chilly outside."

"I'm sorry, what?"

"Your brother and Wellie are out there."

"For goodness' sake," he muttered. "Okay if I let them back in?"

I smiled; I had been the one to suggest it. "Of course."

When they came inside, Wilder rubbed his hands together while Wellie made fun of his inability to handle the cold.

"Where will you stay?" Shiver's brother asked.

"I haven't gotten that far. There's the flat in London, or I was thinking—"

"Not a good idea," said Wilder. "I'll stay at the flat, and you stay in Dorchester House."

"I was going to suggest Dorchester House had you let me finish," Shiver grumbled.

"Where is that?" I asked.

"Here on the estate. It's where Wilder stays when he's here. I'm not around enough to stay anywhere but the main house. At least I didn't use to be."

"We can't put you out."

Wilder put his arm around my shoulders. "You aren't putting me out. I prefer to be in town. The new duke will likely evict me anyway."

Shiver half laughed. "Appreciate this, Wild."

Wellie shook his head and smiled.

"What?" Shiver asked, and I was so glad he did; I was curious to know what Wellie was thinking.

"You'll need to go easy on the duchess, my boy. Her world is a bit different than the one most of us mortals live in. 'Tis not her fault, mind you."

He nodded. "I should go talk to her."

"Darrow too," said Wellie.

"Darrow should go with me, or I should talk to her as well as my mother?"

"The latter, although your sister's time to confront the duchess is not far off."

"Axel is with her now."

Wellie nodded as though he already knew.

I took Kazmir from Shiver's arms, feeling as though I was intruding on their conversation. "I think he might be hungry. I'll just go back to the bedroom."

Wilder, handsome devil that he was, grinned. Pity the poor girl who loses her heart to Shiver's younger brother, I thought, taking in the dimples when he smiled that were so like Kazmir's.

I sat in a chair in the bedroom and settled my baby. My secret was out, and its reveal had been terribly anti-climactic. Shiver wasn't angry, or if he was, he was doing a fantastic job of hiding it. His comments were more about giving me the reasons I should forgive myself for keeping his baby from him.

"Hi," he said, sticking his head in the bedroom door. "Can I come in?"

I rested my head against the back of the chair. "Of course."

"I'll speak with the duchess."

I nodded.

"I'm sorry for making such a mess of it to start with. I should've told her we were coming."

"Why didn't you?"

He shrugged. "I've been telling myself that, now that I'm the duke, I'm my own man who no longer answers to my mother." He laughed. "I sound like a bloody wanker even to myself. If Rivet heard me now, he'd rescind his offer for the top MI6 post."

My eyes opened wide, and I took a deep breath. He'd been offered Rivet's job? Good Lord, what might that mean for Kazmir and me?

"There I go again, putting my foot in it."

"No, it's fine."

"It isn't, but we'll talk more about that later. Now I should be off to see my mother for the second time today and make sure she hasn't contacted the Queen about also rescinding my dukedom."

"Could she?" I gasped.

Shiver laughed. "I don't think so."

31

Shiver

I appreciated the walk to the abbey; I needed time to clear my head and process the earth-shattering, life-altering last few minutes.

Kazmir was my child. In the back of my mind, I'd believed so. It was only the threat of heartache if I were wrong that kept me from accepting it as fact. Everyone around us, it seemed, found it perfectly obvious.

To me, the baby looked more like Losha than anyone in my family, but even Gunner, the last man on earth I would've predicted I'd be having such a conversation with, had said he thought Kazmir looked like me, *his father.*

As I walked, I surveyed the estate. The lawns were covered with a fine dusting of snow, and the gardens were dormant, but the grounds were no less beautiful to me as I walked from Wellie's cottage, past Darrow's Covington House, and past Dorchester House, where Losha and I would reside temporarily.

Each of those structures was a mini-version of the main abbey, designed in the same style with a central entrance and symmetrical wings connected via porticos. The stone used for their construction was the same almost-white alabaster which to some may look cold, but never had to me. The warmth of the light streaming from the windows, whether it was a reflection of the sunlight or the glow of lamps in the evening, had always felt welcoming.

The ponds where I'd frolicked in the water as a child and ice-skated in the winter beckoned me to walk across and leave my tracks on the ice. When I was a boy, Wellie would test the surface to see if it was solid enough for my siblings and me to traipse on. To think the duchess had threatened the man's job just because her daughter was involved with his son. Wellie's family had lived here, and knew every inch of this estate, for generations. If anything, the man belonged here more than my mother did.

I shook my head, knowing that I'd have to leave my poor attitude out here on the lawns, or I'd never get the outcome I sought from my impending conversation.

My mother's reaction, odd as it was, was illogical. The woman had recently reminded us about her desire for grandchildren, and yet, when she first saw Kazmir, she'd fled rather than embrace the gift she'd been asking for.

That Losha and I weren't married couldn't possibly be the reason, could it? Was the duchess really that out of touch with the reality of the modern world? I doubted it very much.

Even after the duke's strokes, my mother still maintained an active social calendar, albeit a fraction of what she'd done in the past.

The flat in London where Wilder would stay wasn't the only one the Whittakers owned. Our main London residence, a flat located in Kensington near the palace gates, had been the location of several parties, small and large, when I was a child and teenager.

My parents' friends included the prime minister and several members of the royal family—who had certainly survived scandals far more interesting than Losha and I having a baby out of wedlock.

My phone vibrated in my pocket, and when I pulled it out, I was surprised to see it was Rivet's assistant, Patsy, calling.

"Happy belated Christmas, Pats," I answered.

"Shiver, I'm glad I was able to reach you."

"What's going on?" I asked, startled by her somber tone.

"I'm sorry to bring sad tidings, but I wanted to let you know that Sir Ranald's wife, Anna, has passed."

"I'm sorry to hear that. What can I do?"

"I know the timing couldn't be worse, but we need you here, Shiver."

"Understood." I ran my hand through my hair. "Let me make the arrangements, and I'll let you know when I'll be in."

"I appreciate this."

"Say no more, Pats. It's my job."

"But you're a duke now."

"Doesn't change a thing."

"Yes, sir."

I smiled, imagining that Patsy had just saluted me. "I'll be in touch shortly."

Patsy was right, the timing couldn't be worse. Before I went into the main house, I called Wilder and told him I'd received a call from Rivet's assistant.

"Have they called you in because of Rivet's wife passing?" he asked when he answered the call.

"Affirmative. I need to think this through, Wild. Can you alert Pinch?"

"Will do."

"Give me thirty minutes, and we'll meet at Dorchester House."

"Understood, Shiv."

"How are Losha and Kazmir getting on with Wellie?"

"They'll be adopted within the hour. Although it's hard to say which one will be the adoptee. Wellie is definitely in full-grandfather mode."

It warmed my heart to hear it. It wasn't that my parents were cold or unloving, but they weren't as open and affectionate as Wellie had always been with us. I didn't remember Pinch's mother; she died when her son was quite young, maybe even still a toddler. Wellie had never remarried, but he was as fine a father as he could be to his only son.

I took a deep breath and opened the front door of Whittaker Abbey, prepared for whatever the duchess hurled at me.

Twenty minutes of searching the house for her later, I went into the garage to see if she'd gone out.

"Yes, sir," reported Thomas. "The duchess left at least thirty minutes ago."

"Did she say where she was going?"

"To town, sir."

"What the bloody hell?" I muttered, walking out of the garage. I felt a bit like a juggler with too many balls in the air. I'd gone from an MI6 agent, bachelor, and marquess, to a duke, father, and next in line to run Section 6 of British Military Intelligence, in less than two months. The enormity of the change in my responsibilities was staggering. It wasn't that I didn't believe myself up to the challenge, I just wished I'd had even a few more days to get used to it all.

I went back to Dorchester House and waited for Wilder and Pinch to arrive.

"How'd it go with the duchess?" asked Wilder, walking in the front door.

"It didn't."

"Meaning?"

"She went to town."

"Do you know why?" my brother asked.

I shrugged, wishing I knew.

"What's happening, then?" asked Pinch.

"Rivet's wife, Anna, passed away."

Pinch scrubbed his face with his hand, which seemed curious to me. Had he had many interactions with Rivet? Even I, who had worked with Sir Ranald since the beginning of my career, didn't know that much about the man's personal life.

"What's that about?" asked Wilder, obviously having the same thoughts I was.

"Bugger me," Pinch muttered.

"Come on, tell us what's got you so worked up."

"It's nothing. Sad news for Rivet."

I shook my head, not in the mood to pull information out of Pinch. "Excuse me. Before we get started, I need a minute to check in with Losha. We have a lot to discuss, and once we're into it, it may be an hour or longer before we are finished."

"Do you want me to bring her here?" offered Wilder.

"Thanks, but let me check with her first."

The two men nodded, but both looked perplexed. Pinch had something on his mind, and whatever it was, I hoped that when I returned, he would be ready to talk about it.

"Hi," Losha answered, sounding as though she'd been laughing.

"Having fun?"

"Oh, Shiver. I love Wellie."

"You're not alone in that."

"Your sister is here as well."

"Darrow?"

"Do you have another sister?"

I chuckled. "No, my darling. What does she think of Kazmir?"

"Like everyone, except your mother evidently, she thinks our son is the most beautiful child who's ever graced the earth."

My breath caught when Losha said "our son." It was the first I'd heard the words, and they warmed my heart better than a shot of Wellie's brandy would do.

"Wellie pulled out some photos of you as a baby, Darrow's too. He was right; Kazmir looks a great deal like both you and her. That might have something to do with your sister's high opinion of his looks."

I could hear Darrow and Wellie in the background, laughing along with Losha. How I wished I could let everything else be damned and join them.

I was about to sign off when I saw Wilder leave through the front door, slamming it behind him.

"What the bloody hell?" I said as I had when my mother pulled her disappearing act. "I'll call you back shortly," I told Losha, rushing to go after Wild.

"Let him go," Pinch said from the drawing room.

"What did you tell him?"

"You might want to have a seat."

"Spit it out, Pinch. I'm in no mood."

"I believe your mother may be on her way to see Rivet."

I sat. "Start at the beginning, and make it damn quick."

32

Losha

When I said I thought Kazmir might be hungry again, Wellie made up an excuse to check something outside.

"Can I stay?" asked Darrow.

"Why would you leave?"

She shrugged. "I thought you might like privacy."

"Only if it makes you uncomfortable."

Darrow shook her head. "So my brother really didn't know the baby was his until this afternoon? Is he really that daft? I thought the man was a spy."

"I've been trying to tell him, but every time I planned to, something happened that prevented us from talking."

"He didn't know the minute he saw him?"

"To be honest, a lot of people have said Kazmir looks like me, but I don't see it either."

Darrow bit her bottom lip. "I'm not sure what I'm permitted to ask."

"You can ask whatever you'd like."

"How did you and Thornton meet?"

I laughed.

"What?" pressed Darrow.

"It's a long story."

She punched in the pillow nearest her on the sofa and rested her head on it. "Okay, go."

"I used to work for an organization called United Russia."

Her eyes scrunched. "Are you Russian?"

I nodded.

"You don't sound Russian."

"I've worked hard not to."

"While your accent is very hard to place, I never would've guessed Russian."

"Part of what made me good at my job."

Darrow cringed. "Which was?"

"I was an operative, but primarily an assassin." I wasn't sure what I expected her reaction to be, but I certainly expected the woman to have one. Instead, she rested her head back on the pillow.

"Go on," she said, appearing nonchalant.

"Being able to speak with many different accents or dialects, made my infiltration of enemy organizations far easier."

"You said you used to work for them. Who do you work for now?"

I leaned down and kissed Kazmir's brow. "I am retired."

Darrow smiled. "Okay, but you haven't answered my original question. How did you and my brother meet?"

"I was hired to kill him."

"I see. Well, I guess that didn't happen."

I laughed again. Darrow really wasn't affected at all by what I was telling her, other than being amused. "No, it didn't. What it did do was mark the beginning of the end of my career—almost my life."

"Really?" She sat up and leaned forward with her elbows on the knees. "Why?"

"As evidenced by this little angel, your brother and I had an affair. One that began shortly after we first met, and carried on until UR put a ten-million-dollar bounty out on my head."

"*Oh. My. God. This is fascinating.* Neither Sutton nor Thornton, nor even Axel, will ever tell me *anything*."

"While I love Kazmir with every fiber of my being, I never planned to get pregnant. The last time your brother and I were together, we agreed that for my safety, we needed to end our affair. It wasn't quite that simple…"

She sat back against the pillow and sighed. "Is it ever when men are involved?"

"I suppose not. But it does explain how I was able to keep the child from him."

"Keep going."

"I had already gone into hiding when I realized I was pregnant. Being so made it necessary for me to be more careful, move more often, cover my tracks better. It's one thing for me to protect myself. It was another thing entirely for me to protect my unborn baby. After Kazmir was born, the need to stay underground intensified."

"What happened next?" Darrow asked, eyes wide.

"Shiver negotiated the release of the bounty."

She sat up again. "Wow. You're joking."

"I'm not. He didn't do it alone. Both SIS and the CIA were involved. I don't know all the details, but the person who was offered up in exchange was someone UR wanted far more than me."

"Who was it?"

"A man named Makar Petrov. He had faked his death years before and had been living in America under an assumed identity. That of a man he'd murdered."

"I am in awe of you right now."

"I had nothing to do with it. You should be in awe of your brother."

"Oh, I am. Both of them actually. I wish they could tell me more than they do." She scrunched her brow. "You aren't going to get in trouble with him for telling me this, are you?"

"I haven't told you anything I shouldn't have."

"Okay. Good. Go on, then," Darrow muttered.

"There was another assassin who was on UR's hit list, someone who is a very dear friend of mine. More like a sister." Kazmir fussed, and I moved him to my other breast. "Anyway, Shiver, along with some other people he works with Stateside, was able to deliver Petrov."

"So United Russia no longer wanted you dead?"

"Oh, they wanted me dead all right. Probably still do, but they stand to lose a great deal of money if they kill me or my friend."

"It must be quite a sum."

"Billions."

"Again, I'm in awe. You're worth *billions* to them?"

"Not at all. It's just part of the deal that was made. Again, nowhere near as simple as the story I'm telling you."

"Understood."

"At first, my excuse for not telling Shiver about the baby was that I was in hiding. He and I had agreed that until we figured out how to make UR's bounty go away, we'd stay out of contact. Once it had been lifted, I stayed on the run. Both because I didn't trust United Russia, and because of my baby."

"You were hiding from Thornton too?"

I nodded. "After Kazmir was born, I was afraid he wouldn't forgive me for keeping him a secret."

"Did he?"

"I suppose you could say that. Your brother vowed to protect us, even before he knew Kazmir was his son."

"He loves you."

"I believe he does."

"Do you love him?"

"With all my heart."

Darrow put her hand on her own heart. "This is the most romantic thing I've ever heard. It should be a book, or better—a movie."

"I don't know about that." I wondered if I was going too far, but given I was here, and likely bringing danger to Shiver's family, I continued. "Shiver found me before your father died. Right after he did, he was called back to London. Once he was gone, someone planted a bomb where I was staying."

Darrow sat straight up, no longer smiling or laughing. It was almost as though she had a personality change. "You and Kazmir could've been killed."

She didn't pose it as a question, but I nodded anyway. "We don't know who was behind it, and that's why I'm here."

"My brother won't let anything happen to the two of you. You know that. He'll die first."

Those were the words he'd used, not that I would tell Darrow that. There was no reason to; she knew her brother.

"Tell me what happened with our mother?"

I shrugged. "I got the impression she didn't want us here. Perhaps she disapproves."

"Yeah, well, I've got you beat. I'm sleeping with the groundskeeper's son. Which reminds me, what's happened to Wellie?"

"I have no idea."

"I'll be right back. I'm going to see if he's still outside. It's bloody cold, not that he'd think so."

"He's asleep," I whispered, looking at my baby.

"I'll be right back," Darrow whispered too.

33

Shiver

By the time Pinch told me what he'd told Wilder, I was ready for a drink.

"I'm not saying there's anything going on between them. I'm only saying that I believe that's where she went."

I studied the man seated in front of me. Pinch was like a brother to me. I had no reason to doubt a single thing he told me, about anything.

The "friendship" between my mother and Rivet was baffling, and that was an understatement, but there was no reason for me to doubt its validity.

"What did you say that made Wilder angry enough to leave?"

Pinch shrugged. "He didn't let me finish."

That didn't sound like Wilder. Not in the slightest.

I shook my head. "I wish I could spend time unraveling this, but I have far more pressing matters to deal with."

"How can I help?"

"I've been called to London to fill in for Rivet during his bereavement leave. Prior to Patsy's call, my intention was to keep Losha and Kazmir here with me, but now I won't be here."

"You don't want them to go to London with you?"

"Not particularly. It makes it far more difficult to ensure their safety. It would require twenty-four-hour protection, along with limited movement. Here, at least, the round-the-clock protection isn't as obvious." I didn't need to explain; Pinch had been the one to set up the security in advance of our arrival.

"You could commute."

I'd thought of that, but with over an hour each way, plus the inconsistent hours I'd need to be at SIS headquarters, I'd have very little time with Losha and Kazmir as it was.

"Have you talked to Rivet?"

I shook my head. "Patsy is the one who called and asked me to come in." If what Pinch said was right and the duchess did go to town to see Rivet, then I definitely didn't want to call him. "We need Wilder back here."

"I'm here," said Wild, walking into the drawing room of Dorchester House.

"What the bloody hell?" I asked, getting really tired of hearing those words come out of my own mouth.

Wilder walked over to Pinch. "I'm sorry, mate. Wasn't anything you said. I mean it was, but I wasn't angry with you."

"What were you angry about?"

"Don't we need to talk about Losha and the baby, Shiv?"

"The more I think about it, my only option is to take them to London with me. Is the duchess staying in the Kensington flat?"

"I would have no way of knowing for certain, but that would be my assumption," my brother answered.

"Better to stay as close as possible to SIS headquarters anyway," suggested Pinch.

"I'll get with MI5 about security, with Pinch's help, of course," said Wilder. "Shiv, you should focus on getting Losha and the baby ready to leave as soon as possible."

"I need to make arrangements with her."

"She's enjoying her time with Wellie so much."

"Darrow too," said Pinch, holding up his phone that displayed a photo of Losha, Kazmir, and Darrow.

How much simpler would it be if we just stayed here? If I resigned from MI6, and Losha and I spent our lives at Whittaker Abbey, raising Kazmir and any other children we were blessed with? We could be happy here; I was certain of it.

Pinch offered to locate Thomas on his way out to let him know not to bother unloading the limousine since we'd be leaving within the hour. Wilder said he'd ride with me, followed by Pinch, and that the entire entourage would be escorted by the security team.

"Did you know Thomas had a family?"

Wilder didn't respond, but his look was questioning.

I ran my hand through my hair. "What if I'm not cut out to take over Rivet's spot?"

"Where's this coming from?" Wild asked, closing the door without going out. "And what does it have to do with Thomas?"

"The duke always made it a point to get to know the people who lived and worked at the abbey."

"If that's all it is, don't make too much of it. I believe the man you're referring to is part of the security team sent in by MI5."

"It isn't just that. I feel out of sorts, as though what I really want to do is walk away from all of SIS and do what Father did—live a simple life here at Whittaker Abbey."

"There's nothing to say you can't do that, Shiv."

"And leave everyone, Rivet included, in the lurch?"

"Maybe not right away, but once things are settled, hand in your resignation."

"Wilder, I need you to tell me what Pinch said that made you so angry."

My brother walked over to the window. "It wasn't what Pinch said. In fact, I think he's a bit off base."

I folded my arms.

"I heard the duchess on the phone earlier. It was right after I saw her and she looked as though she'd seen a ghost."

"And?"

"I didn't know then, but now I believe she was talking to Rivet."

"What did you hear her say?"

"That they had to find 'him,' that it was imperative. She also said that with Anna's death, he no longer had an excuse to wait."

"That's how you knew Anna passed."

Wilder nodded.

"When the duke told me to find someone named Matthew, the words he used were 'before it's too late.'"

"I believe our mother's mysterious and hasty departure may have something to do with this Matthew."

"Me too," I murmured, wondering what my next move should be.

"Perhaps you should revise your plan."

"How so?"

"You and I go to London and find the duchess. If she is with Sir Ranald, we force them to tell us who Matthew is and why the duke was worried enough that his dying words were to find him."

"What about Losha and the baby?"

"They stay here, Shiver. Have Pinch stay too, along with whatever security team he has in place."

"What if I'm required to stay in London?"

"It's an hour's drive to return to Whittaker Abbey, pack them up, and head back to London, security detail with us."

"I hate leaving them here without me."

"I get it, but we won't be gone that long."

I rubbed the ache in the center of my chest. Something felt off. Very much so. I only prayed that whatever it was, related solely to the man my father told me to find, and whom Wilder believed he overheard the duchess discussing with Rivet.

34

Losha

I knew something was wrong the minute Shiver walked in Wellie's front door. Darrow sensed it too; I could tell by the way the woman's arms, currently holding my baby boy, tightened.

"Losha, can I speak with you for a moment?"

"Of course," I said, standing to join him.

"Darrow, will you be okay with the baby for a few minutes?" Shiver asked.

His sister nodded.

Even Wellie's eyes were wide as I followed Shiver out the front door.

"What's happened?"

"Rivet's wife has passed, and I've been called to London."

"I see. How long will you be gone?"

"Only a few hours."

I reached out and rested my hand on his sternum. "Tell me what's really going on, Shiv."

"I'm not certain yet," he said, putting his hand on mine. "You're cold. Let's go 'round back."

He led me through a garden gate and into a small structure I hadn't noticed before.

"What's this?" I asked.

Shiver turned on a light and looked around, seemingly surprised. "I didn't realize he used it," he mumbled, looking at all the paintings hanging on the walls and canvases sitting on easels.

"Is the work Wellie's?" I asked.

Shiver nodded, focusing his attention back on me. "I'm sorry, Losha, but what I have to tell you is quite urgent."

"Go ahead."

"My father's last words to me were about someone he called Matthew. He told me he'd made a mistake, gotten it wrong, and told me to find him."

"You have no idea who he was referring to?"

"None whatsoever." Shiver took a deep breath. "When I went to the abbey to speak with my mother, she wasn't there. According to Thomas, she'd left a few minutes earlier to go to London."

I stepped closer to him. "Tell me the rest, Shiver."

"Wilder overheard her talking to Rivet. While she didn't use the name Matthew, Wild did hear her say that they had to find someone, that it was imperative. My brother also heard her say that now that Anna had passed, Rivet no longer had an excuse to wait."

"Who have you spoken with about this?"

"Only Wilder and Pinch. Until now."

"Perhaps you should ask Wellie."

"I asked him once before, but he wasn't forthcoming."

"Maybe it would be worth trying again."

"I will do." Shiver looked at his phone. "I'm sorry. I need to go, but I'll be back as quickly as I can be."

"Shiver?"

"Yes?"

When I put my arms around his waist, he rested his hands on my shoulders.

"Every time I decide it's time for me to tell you how I feel, one of us—usually you—immediately gets called away. I can't let you leave this time without you knowing…"

He took a deep breath and closed his eyes.

"I love you, Thornton Whittaker, with all my heart. It's always been you. It's only been you."

He opened his eyes and looked into mine. "Losha—"

"Shh," I whispered, bringing my fingertips to his lips. "Let me say it to you this time." I kissed him, deepening it when he opened his mouth to mine. "Hurry back to me, Shiver."

He closed his eyes once more and looked up at the ceiling. "When I get back...line up the child watchers. At least a couple of days' worth."

"Godspeed, Shiv."

"I mean this in the best possible way, Losha..."

I waited for him to continue.

"I've instructed Pinch not to let you and Kazmir out of his sight. Please cooperate."

I nodded. "Understood."

"Thank you."

Shiver held my hand as we walked around the cottage to the front door. Before we went inside, he gripped my neck and ran his thumb over my lips. "I can't do it, Losha. I can't leave without saying it. Don't make me."

I smiled and kissed his fingertips.

"I love you so much, and I love Kazmir too."

"And we love you." Now that I'd said it once, I didn't want to stop telling him what I'd held in my heart far too long.

"You should know that there's a security team in place on the estate."

"I know."

He laughed. "Of course you do."

"Shiver, seriously."

"You've probably been more aware of them than I have. God, I hate to leave," he groaned, kissing me again.

"If you don't leave now, I'm not going to let you go at all."

"One kiss from Kaz before I do. Is that okay? Kaz?"

"You're his father, you can call him whatever you want to."

When we walked in the front door of Wellie's cottage, Kazmir sounded like he'd just gotten fussy. I started toward Darrow to get him, but then hung back. I watched my baby boy's face light up as soon as he saw his father, reaching out for Shiver to pick him up.

My eyes filled with tears seeing him kiss both of our son's cheeks and whisper something in his ear. He walked toward me and kissed the baby one more time before handing him to me.

"I love you," he said, looking at both of us.

"We love you."

Shiver closed his eyes again and sighed. "I must go."

If I kissed him again, I'd only delay his coming back to us, so I turned away. "Go," I pleaded, "or we won't let you."

I walked to the back bedroom to nurse Kazmir, but more because I wanted to be alone to process what had just happened between Shiver and me. I didn't want to share this moment with anyone but my baby boy.

"I love your father with all my heart, Kazmir. Do you understand, my sweet, sweet boy? And your daddy and I love you more than anything else on the face of this earth."

Kazmir studied me and then gave me one of his beloved smiles before resting his head on my chest.

"Losha?" I heard Pinch say a few minutes later, and remembered my promise not to leave his sight.

"I'm here," I said, switching the light on. "I just needed a moment."

"We'll be staying at Dorchester House tonight."

I nodded and stood, soothing Kazmir back to sleep when he fussed. "Darrow?"

"Would you like her at the house as well?" Pinch asked.

"I suppose it's up to her."

He smiled. "Just try to keep her away from that baby."

"Wellie," I said when we walked from the hallway into the main part of the cottage. "Thank you so much for your hospitality and for taking such good care of Kazmir and me."

"You are welcome here anytime, lass. You and the bairn."

"I appreciate it so much."

"Good night, Wellie," said Darrow, kissing his cheek.

"We'll talk later, Dad," said Pinch, squeezing Wellie's shoulder.

"Wait, Axel. Do you have a minute?"

"Not really."

"I can take Losha and the baby over to Dorchester House," offered Darrow. "I'll just swing by Covington and grab a few things."

"It's okay," I told Pinch when I saw him looking back and forth between his father and me. "We'll meet you there."

35

Shiver

"This is the hardest thing I've ever done," I said to Wilder after we were over an hour into our drive.

"You'll have to leave them from time to time, my brother."

"Something isn't sitting right with me."

"What do you mean?"

"In my gut, Wild. I didn't feel as though I should leave tonight. I still don't."

"Listen, we're almost to the Kensington flat. If the duchess is there, we'll have a quick chat and head straight back."

"Right."

More and more, I wondered how I could possibly stay on at MI6. Even if I took Rivet's job, the hours would be long and there would be times I'd have to be away for extended periods of time. I couldn't imagine being away from Losha and Kazmir for a few hours, let alone days.

As far as I knew, Rivet and Anna had only one child, a boy, but I didn't know much about him, even his name. That was telling in itself. I wouldn't be able to compartmentalize as easily as my boss had. If I wasn't with them, I'd likely be talking about Losha and Kaz to whomever would listen.

"Duchess," said Wilder, answering his phone. "Where are you?"

I couldn't hear what she was saying.

"We're on our way there now," Wilder said before hanging up.

"Is she at the flat?" I asked.

"On her way. Should be there by the time we are."

I pulled out my phone. "I'll just check in," I muttered.

My calls to Losha, Darrow, and Pinch all went unanswered. Finally, Wellie picked up.

"They left here about thirty minutes ago," he reported.

"Who did?"

"Losha, Darrow, and the baby. Axel left a few minutes after them."

What the bloody hell? I'd specifically told Pinch not to let her out of his sight. "Where are they now?"

"I think they were headed to Dorchester House."

"Thanks, Wellie. If you happen to hear from Axel, can you please ask him to contact me immediately? It's urgent I speak with him."

"I will, Thornton."

I was about to hang up when Losha's suggestion came to me. "Hey, Wellie?"

"I'm here."

"I asked you once before about someone named Matthew. I'm asking again. What do you know of him?"

Wellie took a deep breath. "Have you spoken with the duchess about this?"

"We're on our way to her now."

"It's better if she's the one to tell you, Thornton."

I pulled the phone away from my ear, incredulous. "He hung up. He bloody hung up."

"What did he say about Matthew?"

"That it's best if the duchess tells us who he is. At least that's what I think he meant."

In all the years I'd known him, this was the first time Wellie cut me off. The bad feeling I'd had since before I left Whittaker Abbey intensified ten-fold.

By the time we walked in the door of our mother's flat, I was furious.

"Who's Matthew?" I asked before we'd even said hello.

"Thornton—"

"Who is he, Duchess?"

"Shiver…" Rivet came around a corner. "Please have a seat."

"Not until you tell me who Matthew is and why my father's dying words were for me to find him."

When the duchess gasped, Rivet walked over and put his hand on her shoulder.

"Who is he, Rivet?"

"Matthew is my son. Mine and Anna's."

"Not good enough. I asked you a specific question, and I expect an answer."

"Thornton—"

I held up my hand. "I've run out of patience with the both of you. I want you to sit down, this minute, and explain to me why my father told me to find him."

My mother's eyes filled with tears, and Rivet looked as though he might tear his hair out with the way he was running his hand through it.

"Enough with the secrets. Get on with it."

"It isn't an easy story to tell, Thornton," said the duchess, dabbing her tears with a handkerchief. "Your father was involved with another woman before he and I were married."

I immediately saw where this was going, but under no circumstances would I relent. Between my mother and Rivet, I expected to hear the full story.

"That woman was my wife, Anna," said Rivet, now seated next to the duchess.

"Shortly before your father and I were to be married, Anna discovered she was pregnant." She looked at Rivet, and he rested his hand on hers.

How had Rivet gotten involved in this whole sordid affair, and what was his relationship with my mother?

Rivet's gaze met mine. "Anna and I were married within the month."

"Arranged by whom?"

"Me," answered the duchess.

"Why?"

"The answer should be obvious."

"If it were obvious, I wouldn't ask. Why did you arrange a marriage between the duke's mistress and Sir Ranald?" I saw my mother cringe, but I was beyond caring.

"Your father was destined to be the next Duke of Bedfordshire—the heir to one of the great estates in all of England."

"Surely, you didn't ask Ranald to marry a complete stranger because of an estate, Mother."

"As much as you're inclined to walk away from your birthright, your father was not. I didn't act alone, Thornton. I offered assistance at your grandparents' request."

"We aren't living in the eighteenth century, Duchess," added Wilder. "Having a child out of wedlock, even having a mistress, is not a reason for someone to give up their birthright."

The duchess folded her arms. "And what of Charles and Diana?"

Wilder rolled his eyes and paced to the other side of the room. "Jesus," he muttered.

"Charles had been involved with another woman—a married woman—for years, and yet he married someone the palace approved of, not the woman he loved."

"Our father was a duke, not the bloody future King of England," Wilder spat.

There were several things about my mother's last statement that bothered me. One, that she believed her role in arranging for Rivet to marry a woman who was a stranger to him, pregnant with another man's child, was her duty as the future duchess. Second was her comparison of the situation to the current Prince of Wales' relationships. Had my father loved this Anna? Had he married my mother because she was someone of whom his parents approved? Had she arranged for the marriage solely to secure her ongoing position in English society?

"Why, Ranald?"

I knew I'd hit a nerve when my mother looked at Rivet once again. There was love between them. I couldn't say for certain it was romantic love, but there was an affection that ran deep.

"I volunteered."

Of course Rivet would shield the duchess from having to answer.

"How were you compensated for this union?"

"Thornton!" my mother gasped.

"It's okay, Victoria. It's a logical question for him to ask."

"One I expect an answer to," I told them.

"Both of us do," added Wilder.

"Your father played an integral role in gaining my employment with SIS."

"What about the knighthood?" Wilder asked.

"The duke had nothing to do with that."

"Was Wilder's and my employment with SIS part of this arrangement?"

"Neither were," Rivet answered.

"Why did my father tell me to find Matthew?"

"My wife suffered from Borderline Personality Disorder as does her son."

"Where is he presently?"

"I don't know."

"Why did my father tell me to find him 'before it was too late'?"

"And why did I overhear you say that now that Anna was dead, Rivet no longer had an excuse to wait?" added Wilder.

Again, Rivet answered for the duchess. "As for Anna, she begged me not to go after Matthew. She knew that if I did, he might be incarcerated. With her as sick as she was...my focus was primarily on her care. As for why your father told you to find him before it was too late, I can't say for certain, but I believe he may have attempted to get in touch with the duke."

"It was right after the first stroke. I believe Matthew's demands may have triggered the others," the duchess interjected.

"What demands?" I asked.

For the third time, my mother looked at Rivet before responding.

"He wanted to be named rightful heir," she said only after Rivet nodded.

"Did he make any threats?" asked Wilder.

"He did."

When I saw my brother stalking toward Rivet, I intercepted him. "Whatever you intend to do, I implore you not to."

"Why not? You heard him. Our father's illegitimate son is a sociopath who made threats against our family."

"Sutton, Matthew is mentally ill—"

Wilder turned on our mother. *"Are you defending him?"*

"Why haven't you apprehended him?" I asked before the duchess had a chance to respond.

"There wasn't enough of a credible threat that would've allowed us to."

Wild shook his head in disgust. "And yet you believe these threats triggered our father's series of strokes."

"I don't know for certain, Sutton."

I grabbed the back of the chair in front of me when the ramifications of this conversation dawned on me. "Do you have any reason to believe that Matthew had anything to do with the bomb that almost killed Losha and our son?"

Rivet didn't need to answer. I saw it in his eyes.

"You bloody *sonuvabitch*," I seethed. As much as Wilder had wanted to attack the man only moments ago, it took all of my self-restraint not to do so myself. "I couldn't reach her," I muttered. "I couldn't fucking reach her."

"What are you saying?" asked Wilder.

"Losha—I couldn't reach her. *Is the man in England?*"

"It is possible."

I got right in his face when Rivet stood. "You better fucking pray that there is a good explanation as to why I was unable to reach the mother of my child, my sister, nor the man that I entrusted with her and my son's well-being. If anything has happened to them, not only will I kill this Matthew, you'll be next on my list."

The duchess got between Rivet and me. "Thornton, I will not allow this kind of talk."

I glared at her. "Stay out of this, Mother. This is none of your concern."

"Can't you see this may be for the best? Isn't it obvious that the sins of the father are repeating with the son?"

I took two steps back, trying to reconcile the words my mother had just spoken. Had she actually suggested that something happening to my son and his mother would be for the best?

"Wait, Thornton, I didn't mean that in the way it sounded," she cried. "I didn't mean something should happen to the child."

I could barely look at her. Whether she'd meant her words in the way they sounded or not, she was, in some way, alluding that my being the father of an illegitimate baby was a sin. As Wilder had said earlier, we weren't living in the eighteenth century. To think that my own father had allowed another man to marry the mother of his firstborn child was something I couldn't fathom any more than what my mother had just said to me.

"We have to go," I said to Wilder. *"Now."*

Wild was ahead of me, but turned to address Rivet. "Whatever resources there are from any section of SIS, they need to be on their way to Whittaker Abbey immediately."

"I'll take care of it," answered Rivet.

"You best pray this is a false alarm, and nothing has happened to them. If something has, I'll kill you with my bare hands before Shiver has the chance." Wilder turned to our mother. "And you, Duchess, best think long and hard about what you just suggested. Like Shiver, if anything has happened to Losha or the baby, I will also hold you personally responsible."

"But that isn't what I meant…"

I heard my brother's words and the cries of my mother, but I couldn't stop to process them. Losha and the baby were in grave danger; I felt certain of it.

Rivet followed us to the lift. "Before you go, here is his likeness." He handed me a photograph.

"*This* is Matthew?"

Rivet nodded. "Do you recognize him?"

I handed the photo to Wilder who shook his head. "Looks familiar, but I can't place him."

I studied the image a second time. "How recent is this?"

"Not more than a couple of years."

"He looks…*Jesus! It's Thomas,*" I exclaimed, punching the buttons on the lift.

"Let me see that again," said Wilder, holding out his hand. "It *is* him."

"Who is Thomas?" I heard my mother ask from inside the flat.

"The driver."

36

Losha

I was laughing at something Darrow said as I followed her into Covington House, so when Shiver's sister came to a dead stop, I ran right into the back of her, pinning Kazmir between us.

"Sorry," I mumbled, taking a step back and then looking up to see the gun pointed directly at the woman's temple.

I heard a man's voice telling Darrow to move and then saw him yank her arm. Before I could turn and flee, the same gun was pointed at my baby boy.

"Stop right where you are!" the man, who looked vaguely familiar, shouted at me, and I froze. *"Get inside,"* he demanded, waving the gun but not enough that I could take action.

My eyes met Darrow's, and I slowly shook my head, praying she wouldn't do anything foolish. It was too dangerous for either of us to try to thwart a man with a gun trained on my son.

"Sit there!" the man shouted at us.

We sat side by side on a sofa, with Kazmir on my lap. My phone vibrated in my pocket.

"Don't touch it!" the man yelled.

Within moments, the same thing happened with Darrow's phone.

I quickly surveyed the room while he stood a few feet from us. The only houses I'd been in on the estate were the abbey and Wellie's cottage. It was unlikely the layout of this one was similar to either. Planning an escape route after first figuring out how to disarm the man with the gun, would be impossible.

My next concern was Pinch. He was either on his way here or going directly to Dorchester House. If it was the latter, then he would likely circle back here when we didn't arrive as planned.

Whoever had called, whether it was Shiver, Pinch, or someone else, would be on high alert after not being able to reach me or Darrow.

Between Wellie's cottage and here, I hadn't seen signs of the security team I had already been aware of before Shiver told me about them. Wasn't there supposed to be eyes on me and Kazmir at all times? Were they somehow in on this?

I studied the man, knowing I'd seen him recently, but I couldn't place him.

"Who are you?" asked Darrow.

"None of your concern," he spat.

"What do you want of us?"

"You'll learn that soon enough."

"If it's money you want, I can arrange for a ransom, and for your safe passage," she offered.

"Silence!" the man shouted at Darrow and shook his head. "You offer money that doesn't belong to you. It belongs to *me*. Do you understand? It's *mine*."

"Matthew," I whispered.

"What did you say?" he shouted at me.

"You're Matthew."

"Don't pat yourself on the back too hard, *Losha*."

"Where have we met before?"

"No talking!" the man shouted, waving the gun at us.

"If it isn't money you want, what is it?"

"I want what should have been mine all along."

I suddenly realized where I recognized the man from. When I'd seen him before, he'd had dark sunglasses on and I'd only seen him for brief moments, mainly from behind. "The driver," I muttered, immediately wishing I hadn't said it out loud.

The man's crow-like cackle sent shivers up my spine. "A hired driver, like a servant, on an estate that is *my* birthright."

"Who are you?" asked Darrow. "Why do you think you have any claim on Whittaker Abbey?"

The man moved closer, getting almost in Darrow's face. The only thing stopping me from acting was that his gun was pointed at my precious son. I pulled Kazmir closer, praying the baby wouldn't do anything to further anger the man.

"Who am I?" he seethed. "I am your oldest brother. The rightful heir to Whittaker Abbey. The man who should now, and will soon be, the duke."

"If you're the heir, why haven't my brothers or I ever met you?"

"Because your bitch of a mother married the duke when my own mum should've been the next duchess."

What Darrow was doing was exactly what I had been trained to do. The hostage appealing to the human side of the would-be assassin.

I kept my focus riveted on the man, looking for any sign that I could overwhelm him and take his gun.

I heard a sound from outside that the man had obviously noticed as well.

"Silence!" he shouted a second time, and to my horror, Kazmir began to wail.

37

Shiver

Thoughts ran through my mind so fast, I couldn't focus. I tried again to reach Losha, then Darrow, and finally, Pinch. All to no avail. The list of people I'd kill if anything happened to her or our child, grew by the minute.

When my phone buzzed, I almost went through the roof of Wilder's car.

"Please, please, please be Losha," I pleaded, but it wasn't. It was Pinch, and he was the second on the list of people I prayed I'd hear from.

"Pinch—"

"Shiver, we have a code black—Losha and Darrow are being held captive, and we can't get to them."

"Why the fuck not?"

"He's got explosives set up all around Covington House. Dorchester too."

I wanted to scream at Pinch, ask why the hell he'd let them out of his sight in the first place, but Pinch's focus couldn't be on answering my questions. His mind had to be on how to rescue the most important people on earth to me.

"Where's Pimm?" I asked Wilder, who immediately placed the call to find out.

"We've lost several operatives, Shiv. He's taken out at least ten, maybe more. Our radios are down. It all seemed to happen at once."

"We're on our way back, another forty-five minutes out." *Why the hell hadn't it dawned on me to go by heli? Jesus.*

"Wilder is contacting Pimm. Rivet is sending the full force of SIS." Although, without radio communication, it would be impossible for Pinch to let them know the kind of help he needed.

"I've got Pimm," said Wilder.

"Hold on, Pinch."

I grabbed Wilder's phone. "Pimm, please tell me you're in the UK, preferably in London."

"Better than that. I was already on my way to Bedfordshire. I'll arrive in less than ten."

"Thank God. The radio system is down. Call Pinch on his cell."

"Understood."

I ended the call with Pimm on Wilder's phone and placed another call to Rivet. As much as I hated the fact that I had to rely on him, I had no choice.

"Here's what I know so far, and here's what I need you to do."

When I finished briefing Rivet, I picked up my call with Pinch.

"Pimm just arrived. I'll ring you back, Shiv."

"What's happening?" Wilder asked when I tossed my cell on the seat.

I told him about the explosives and the fallen operatives.

"How the hell did one man arrange all of this in an hour's time?"

I shook my head. Best guess? He'd been planning something like this since before the duke fell ill. God knew how the man got MI5 credentials—obviously Rivet had no knowledge he had.

In the last twenty-four hours, he'd had free access to Losha, our baby, Pinch, and me. He'd been able to follow everything that was happening in real time since he'd made himself the main contact at the garage.

"He's fucking sick," said Wilder, mirroring my thoughts exactly. "What's his plan, Shiver?"

"To take us all out, Wild."

"My thoughts precisely."

When Wilder and I arrived at Whittaker Abbey less than an hour later, a command center had been set up and Pimm was briefing the agents Rivet had sent on how to diffuse the explosives. I listened, thanking God when I heard Pimm say it had to be done in such a way that the alert system would not notify the bomb's maker of its diffusion.

The man had drawn out where we needed to start and what components we needed to leave in place.

"We'll go to Covington House first," said Pimm. "The second team will be on standby at Dorchester."

I nodded and motioned for Pinch and Wilder to follow me.

"As soon as Pimm gives the word, this is how we'll go in."

38

Losha

I held Kazmir as close to me as I could while our captor checked his phone.

"It won't be long now," he said, smiling down at us. "Everything is going as planned."

The only way I knew to keep Kazmir quiet was to nurse him. I shifted him to my breast, covered myself, and said a silent prayer that he'd drift to sleep.

My eyes met Darrow's. Shiver's sister was holding it together well, but how much longer would she be able to?

"What will you do to us?" Darrow asked.

"It's quite simple, really. They're aware you're here and still alive. They'll come, thinking they can save you, but what they don't know is that I've been planning this since I was a lad."

I gave a slight head nod to Darrow. The more she could get him to tell us, the better we'd be able to act when given the opportunity.

"What will happen when they come for us?"

"Kaboom!" shouted Matthew, jarring Kazmir awake. I eased him back on the breast before he could fuss.

"What's the point, then?" Darrow asked.

"Come again."

"Seems obvious to me, Matthew. 'Kaboom,' as you said, means we all blow up. Wouldn't it have been easier to just introduce yourself to my brother than kill yourself?"

"No, no, no," he laughed. "I will be long gone by the time they've crossed the threshold. And then, without a living heir, I will simply submit my DNA and, as I've said, everything that rightfully belongs to me shall be mine."

Darrow shook her head and laughed. "I guess you haven't been read in on my brother's meetings with the solicitor."

I watched the man turn his back on Darrow, at first, seeming as though he was disinterested in what she was saying.

"About what?"

"The trust, of course. Thornton has no interest in Whittaker Abbey. He never has. Neither Sutton nor I have either. Upon the duke's death, Thornton had his trust rewritten, giving the estate in its entirety back to the crown, as it were, as so many in our position have been forced to do. The income will never be what it once was, and the taxes, well, they could bankrupt us inside of the first year."

"You're lying."

Darrow shrugged. "All of this for nothing," she said. "Such a shame."

"Silence!" he shouted again as he paced in front of the window.

He wasn't afraid of being seen. In fact, he wanted to be. He must have some kind of trigger set to alert him when someone crossed the outer parameter, at which point, he'd leave through the only safe passage out of the house. Once whoever was coming in after us crossed the second parameter, whatever explosives he'd put into place, would detonate, killing us all.

Anyone analyzing the situation would assume it was a simple hostage negotiation. They would have no idea that, instead, the man who held us captive had been planning something this elaborate for years.

I'd said few prayers in my lifetime, and those I had were always for the safety of my precious Kazmir.

Tonight I prayed not only for him, but for myself and his father, Darrow, Wilder, Pinch, and even Wellie. God save our souls if not our lives.

39

Shiver

I watched Pimm as he painstakingly separated wires, reattaching them just as carefully.

"That's it," he said, looking up at me. "You're in."

"You're sure?"

Pimm had reprogrammed the device's detonation protocol so it neither alerted a system failure nor a parameter breach. As far as Matthew Caird knew, everything was working the way he'd initially set it up.

"It's the same way the house in California was wired. Two parameters, although the first was simply an alert. It's the second that was intended to trigger the detonation."

"Didn't you say that bomb was programmed to detonate at three in the morning?"

"Only as a backup."

"What do you mean?"

"When Losha stepped over the threshold of the stairwell, the device should have detonated."

"*Jesus,* it was a mistake?"

"I'm afraid so, sir."

I thought back to the way I'd walked the cottage on Butler Ranch, checking each entrance, all the windows, and finally, the basement. I hadn't done so at the beach house. "He expected me to stay. I was supposed to be the one who crossed the second parameter."

Pimm nodded.

"Shiv? Are you ready?" asked Wilder.

"Radios?"

"Affirmative," said Pinch, handing me a headset.

"Is the communication system functional?"

"Completely."

Rivet had delivered more than I'd asked for, and while I appreciated it, whether I could forgive the man for his lies by omission, remained to be seen. If I had to make a decision today, I wouldn't just leave MI6 and SIS; I fully intended to leave the UK entirely—once Losha, Kazmir, and Darrow were safe, and Matthew Caird was either apprehended or dead. Admittedly, I'd prefer the latter.

I looked into Pimm's eyes and put my hand on the man's shoulder. "My son is in there."

Pimm nodded. "Go get him."

We'd agreed that Pinch would go in through the basement, Wilder would stand at the ready near the front door, and I would gain access through the back door of the house.

At my signal, Pinch would cut the main power from the electrical box in the basement and the lights would go out. At that point, I would be close enough to take the man down, neutralizing him by whatever means necessary.

All three of us activated our night vision devices and waited for me to give the signal to go.

I took a deep breath, knowing this was the single-most important op of my life. Nothing that had come before and nothing that might come after would ever be of equal measure to saving the lives of my child, the woman who held my heart, and my sister.

With a nod of my head, we each went in a different direction. In less than a minute, I was inside, listening to my sister tell the man who threatened all their lives that the estate he claimed as his rightful inheritance would soon belong to the crown. Her voice sounded confident and condescending, rattling the man just enough to distract him.

I crept through the mudroom and kitchen, like the ghost I was known to be. I stopped less than five feet from Caird, who had no idea I was within killing range.

I pressed a button on the headset, which sent the message to Pinch to kill the house's power.

40

Losha

Before the end of my prayer, I knew it had been answered. I couldn't see or even hear Shiver, but I felt him. He was here, inside, ready to act. With one arm, I secured Kazmir as close to my body as I could. I rested my other hand on the sofa, near Darrow, touching the side of her leg with my pinky.

Darrow blinked three times, letting me know she was on alert.

Within seconds, the electricity in the house was cut and the lights went out.

"Down," I stated simply as Darrow and I slid off the sofa and to the floor. I covered Kazmir's tiny body with mine as I listened to the scuffle that ensued, holding my breath in anticipation of gunfire. Instead, I heard the sound of the gun hitting the floor, followed by the thud of a body doing the same.

The lights came on, and I looked into the most beautifully haunting green-gray eyes I'd ever seen. Silently, Shiver helped me stand while Wilder came in and did the same with Darrow. I watched as Pinch came in from behind us and approached the body of the man who had come so close to killing us all.

"There's a pulse," I heard him murmur as Shiver led Kazmir and me out the front door.

"You didn't kill him?"

"No," he answered simply. "Should I have? I don't know," he whispered, asking and answering his own question.

I couldn't say why I wouldn't have wanted him to, other than I'd do everything to keep my baby boy as far from death as I could.

Once we were outside, beyond the pathway that led from the house, I let the sob loose that I'd held inside since I first saw the barrel of a gun pointed at Darrow. A floodgate of tears opened as I clung to Shiver and our baby.

"Shh," he whispered, holding me and Kazmir close. "You're safe. It's over now, Losha."

"Let's go, Shiv," said Wilder, escorting us along with Pinch and Darrow to a waiting van.

Once inside, we followed another vehicle off the estate grounds. I could tell by the lights reflected in the snow that there was at least one vehicle following us, maybe more.

"What happened to him?" Darrow asked Pinch.

"He's in custody."

"Where are we going?"

"Somewhere safe," he answered.

I closed my eyes and put my hand on Shiver's, both resting near the heart of our son. I was so grateful we weren't staying at the abbey. No matter how many people reassured me otherwise, I wouldn't feel safe.

"Rivet reports we have the entire Lanesborough booked."

I felt Shiver tense.

"Go to the Connaught instead," he instructed his brother.

Wilder nodded.

"Shiv, I'm so sorry—"

"Not now, Pinch."

I wanted to defend Pinch's actions, take responsibility for him staying behind when Darrow and I left Wellie's cottage.

Whether the outcome of what we'd gone through would've been any different, didn't matter. There was a chance that if Pinch had been with us, we'd all be dead. But Pinch didn't answer to me; he answered to Shiver, whose direct orders he'd gone against.

The convoy of vehicles entered through the rear garage entrance. The cars that led and followed pulled up on either side of the elevator bank, while the van we were in pulled directly in front. Shiver took my hand and escorted me out of the vehicle and then stepped back inside to get Kazmir from the car seat someone had thought to have installed. My guess was that it had been Rivet, or someone acting on his orders, and while I appreciated it, I knew now also wasn't the time to ask Shiver why he was making decisions contrary to those made by his boss.

We rode the elevator in silence, and when it reached the top floor, Shiver led me to the right while Darrow, Pinch, and Wilder went in the opposite direction.

Another elevator pinged, and four SIS personnel exited, followed shortly thereafter by another ping and more agents taking various positions on the floor.

"Come, Losha," Shiver said, opening the door to a suite and leading me through the entry and to a chair where I sat and held our sleeping baby.

Once again I broke down, but this time my tears silently slid down my cheeks.

Every few minutes, Shiver would go to the door and I'd hear him directing where the items being delivered were to be placed.

After a while, I dozed off, still sitting in the same chair, still holding our sleeping baby.

I slept on and off for at least an hour, maybe longer, and then stood and carried Kazmir into another room of the suite. I didn't see Shiver right away, but when I heard his voice catch, I found him sitting near the window.

"Shiver?"

He turned his head away from me and brought his hand to his face.

"Kazmir wants his daddy," I said, barely able to hold the baby who was reaching out for him.

"Not now, Losha."

I walked closer and eased the baby onto his lap, so Shiver had no choice but to take him.

"I can't do this," he said.

"What can't you do?"

Shiver stood and handed Kazmir back to me. The baby immediately began to cry, arching his back and reaching again for his father.

I watched him walk to the other side of the room and come to a stop. "I'm leaving tonight."

"I don't understand."

He shook his head but didn't turn around. "I'm sure you will after some time."

"I will not."

Shiver spun around. "I didn't protect either of you. I brought danger to you. You both could've been killed *twice,* solely because of me."

"You saved us."

"No, Losha. Matthew was there to kill me, both in California and then at the abbey. It was only by the grace of God that he didn't murder you and Kazmir instead. I cannot stay. I cannot be a part of your lives. It's too dangerous."

He walked to the door and opened it, pausing before stepping over the threshold. "I'll make arrangements for you to have everything you need. Wherever you choose to live, everything will be paid for. You'll never want for money, Losha." He hesitated and took a deep breath. "I'm sorry. Please know that I will love you both forever."

He walked out, and the door closed behind him as our baby boy wailed, *"Dada!"*

"Darrow, I need you to watch Kazmir," I said when Shiver's sister answered my call. "I'll bring him to you."

"Of course. What's going on?"

"I need to find Shiver."

"What do you mean?"

"He's left us, and I need to find him."

"I'll come to you if it's easier."

I looked about the room. Shiver had made arrangements for a crib and changing table to be delivered along with a portable crib, a high chair, diapers, food, and clothing. "It would be easier."

A few minutes later, I heard a knock at the door. When I looked through the peephole, I saw Wilder and Pinch were with Darrow.

"I'm sorry about Shiv," said Wilder once they were inside. "I won't make excuses, but I know he blames himself."

"Thank you. I understand how he's feeling; I would feel the same way myself. To a certain extent, I already do. If I hadn't insisted you stay and talk to your father, what might have happened?" I said to Pinch. "And if I had let Shiver know I was pregnant straightaway, not kept the baby from him, how would things have worked out differently? And what if Pimm hadn't been able to diffuse the explosives tonight, what would have happened then?" I shook my head. "We have no way of knowing what may or may not have happened. None of us."

The three people standing in front of me nodded.

"Where is he?"

"To be honest, I have no idea," said Wilder.

"Me neither," added Pinch.

"I have a guess," said Darrow.

"Where?" asked her brother.

"He has unfinished business."

"Right. He's with Rivet and the duchess."

41

Shiver

I walked from the hotel to the Kensington flat. With every step, I fought my body's urge to turn around and return to Losha and our baby. The sound of my little boy crying out for me echoed in my head, breaking my heart.

Since the day I'd first met Losha, I'd begun the process that inevitably put her at risk, not just once, but many times.

I'd known she was right, that our relationship was dangerous for her, but I'd insisted, showing up where I knew she'd be, arranging secret trysts.

The bounty placed on her head by United Russia was because of me too; they'd believed she was a double agent, in part due to my relentless pursuit of her.

When the bounty was lifted, I'd been intransigent in my determination to find her, and while I knew I shouldn't, I insisted on spending time with her and her baby, even when I'd believed Kazmir was another man's child.

The entire time, Losha's wishes had remained the same. The only thing she'd wanted was to keep her baby safe.

I'd vowed to protect them and did the opposite. Not only had I endangered their lives, but also that of my own sister.

I was a failure as a father, a man, and a brother. I had no right to ask Losha's forgiveness any more than I could remain in the employ of MI6.

Once I saw Rivet and resigned, and issued an ultimatum to my mother regarding my son and siblings, I'd create a new life for myself. I certainly knew how to do it in a way that no one would ever be able to find me.

I was buzzed into the building without a word. When I exited the elevator on the top floor, both the duchess and Rivet stood waiting.

"Thornton," my mother cried, charging forward to embrace me. "Will you ever forgive me? I've been out of my mind with worry... There is no excuse..."

I took her arms that were around my neck and moved them to her sides. "Let's go inside," I said, nodding at Rivet.

"I'm leaving," I said after telling them to be seated.

"Before I ask where you're going, I'd like to thank you for not killing Matthew. While he wasn't my biological son, I was still the man who raised him," said Rivet.

"As far as Matthew is concerned, don't thank me. I honestly don't know why I didn't kill the bastard. In terms of where I'm going, I don't know where yet, and when I do, no one else will."

Rivet nodded. "Understood."

"As is obvious, I'm resigning my position with MI6." I turned to my mother. "However, that does not mean I intend to spend any time whatsoever at Whittaker Abbey. When I'm ready, I'll have a discussion with Wilder and Darrow as to their wishes about it."

"And what am I to do?"

"Should we decide to relinquish the estate, it will be with the stipulation that you'll be allowed to live out your days in the abbey."

"Thornton—"

I held up my hand. "I have nothing else to say on the matter."

"Can you ever forgive me?"

"I am unable to say so definitively."

The duchess began to cry.

"You suggested to me that my beloved son was somehow a sin. I cannot reconcile those words with the woman who raised me."

"Thornton, I beg you—that's not what I meant."

"Yet that's what you said, and I find it unforgivable."

"What does that mean?"

"It means, Duchess, that for all intents and purposes, my mother died the same day my father did."

When I turned to leave, there, standing just inside the door, was Losha. I had no idea how she'd gained entry or how much she'd heard of what I'd said to my mother or to Rivet.

"Excuse us," I said, taking her arm and leading her out of the flat. "What are you doing here?"

"I would think that's obvious."

"I said all I had to say back at the hotel."

"I'm sure you did."

"Well, then." I pressed the button for the lift, and when it arrived, we both stepped inside.

She stood in front of the control panel and hit the emergency button when the door closed, bringing the lift to a stop. "Now you'll listen to what I have to say."

"Losha—"

"No, Shiver. You'll listen, for now the tables have turned."

"What does that mean?"

"Simply put, if you walk away, I'll come after you. If you hide from me, I'll find you. I'm never letting you go, Shiver. That's a promise I intend to keep for the rest of my life."

"What if I refuse?"

"I won't accept it."

"Why not?"

"Because I love you. Why did you make the same promise to me?"

"Because I love you."

"Our son said his first word today. He said 'Dada.'"

"I heard him, and my heart nearly broke."

"You cannot leave us. You can't. We're a family, Shiver. Let us be a family."

My shoulders fell forward, and Losha put her arms around me.

"Losha, how can you forgive me? How can I forgive myself?"

"By being the best parents we can be to Kazmir, by loving each other no matter what, for the rest of our lives."

"Will that be enough?"

She put her palms on each side of my face. "That is everything. There is nothing more than love, Shiver."

I held her tight to me, praying she was right, praying that she'd find a way to forgive me for not keeping her and our son safe. And more, praying I could forgive myself.

"There's one more thing I need from you, although it won't change the promise I just made to you."

"What's that?"

"I need you to forgive your mother."

"Losha—"

"Hear me out."

I nodded.

"If you don't forgive her, then we can't raise our son, or any other children we have, at Whittaker Abbey."

"I never dreamed you'd want to."

"I do."

"Why?"

"I want our children to grow up surrounded by people who love them. I want them to learn all about the place that has been handed down through your family for generations. I want them to know Wellie and

Darrow and Wilder and Pinch, and even your mother. Someday, I want them to know where I came from too."

"The duchess…"

"Deserves the same forgiveness the rest of us do."

"You don't know—"

"I do."

"How can you forgive her, then?"

"Isn't Kazmir worth forgiving everything, Shiver?"

"I have one request of you."

"Anything."

I smiled.

"Well? What?" she asked when I reached around her and hit the lift's button to take us back to the top floor.

"Come with me," I said, pulling her back to the flat. I knocked and then entered without waiting for either the duchess or Rivet to answer the door.

"Thornton?" said my mother, still seated where she'd been when we walked out.

"I need to speak with Rivet."

"I'm here," he said, coming around the corner.

"I need you to pull some strings for me, and I want you to do it now."

"What's that?"

"Losha needs asylum, and I want you to put a rush on her citizenship papers."

Rivet turned to Losha, who nodded.

"Excuse me," he said, walking back in the direction from where he'd come. A few minutes later, he returned wearing a coat. "Ready?"

"Where are we going?"

"To Number 10. The prime minister is expecting us."

Epilogue

Shiver

"No second thoughts?"

"None."

"We'll be away three entire weeks, Losha."

"I made the reservations, Shiver."

"It's a long while."

"Darrow is perfectly capable of caring for Kazmir while we're away. She'll have help not only from the nanny, but from Wilder, Pinch, Wellie, and even the duchess. Our son will have no shortage of love in our absence."

"Let's board, then."

I led my wife onto the private plane that would carry us to the States for her best friend's wedding, after which we intended to go on a past-due honeymoon of our own.

"The last time we were on this plane, I dreamed of us," I told her.

"What about us?"

"Come with me, and we'll make it come true."

Keep reading for a sneak peek
at the next book in the
the Royal Agents of MI6 Series—
The Lord and the Spy

1

Wren

Wilder Whittaker stood, perhaps waiting for me to do the same, but I wanted to see what he'd do if I didn't. He didn't disappoint.

The swoon-worthy, handsome agent leaned all six feet three inches of his powerful body on the hand he placed on his desk almost close enough to touch my bottom. He moved so I could see his eyes, which looked almost black from a distance, were really brown with flakes of gold and green. His wavy dark-brown hair had strands of blond and maybe even some gray mixed in. But mostly, his scent—a mix of sandalwood, citrus, and something else that smelled almost of aristocracy—filled my nostrils with an undeniable want.

Without needing to reach, I could slide my hand inside the folds of his jacket and run it over what I knew were the rock-hard pectoral muscles in his chest, then to his powerful shoulders, and up to cup his cheek and run my finger over the smirk on his lips.

"I'll see you at eight, Miss Harlow," he breathed, moving closer to me still. "In the meantime, think long and hard about how you want this to play out."

"Meaning?"

"Just because they call me Wild doesn't mean I don't know how to be subdued, controlled, even civilized. Although, I'd far prefer it if you chose adventurous, entertaining—even titillating."

"It's just dinner, Mr. Whittaker."

"It stopped being 'just dinner' the minute you walked into my office. You know it as well as I do."

About the Author

USA Today and Amazon Top 15 Bestselling Author Heather Slade writes shamelessly sexy, edge-of-your seat romantic suspense.

She gave herself the gift of writing a book for her own birthday one year. Forty-plus books later (and counting), she's having the time of her life.

The women Slade writes are self-confident, strong, with wills of their own, and hearts as big as the Colorado sky. The men are sublimely sexy, seductive alphas who rise to the challenge of capturing the sweet soul of a woman whose heart they'll hold in the palm of their hand forever. Add in a couple of neck-snapping twists and turns, a page-turning mystery, and a swoon-worthy HEA, and you'll be holding one of her books in your hands.

She loves to hear from my readers. You can contact her at heather@heatherslade.com

To keep up with her latest news and releases, please visit her website at www.heatherslade.com to sign up for her newsletter.

MORE FROM AUTHOR HEATHER SLADE